3

The Frank Doyle Reports

DEATH IS 27 RED

H E Joyce

H E Joyce

Table of Contents

Chapter One

Six Months Ago.

Hugo's Casino was busy, it always was on a Saturday night. An attraction for residents and tourists alike, the casino was located just South of Boston. It offered hundreds of slot machines, blackjack and two roulette tables; the casino was a thoroughly legal business. Thousands of dollars could be lost on any night by clients who walked through their doors.

David Ryan was no exception. He was in his mid-thirties, had a good job and was well-paid, renting a pleasant apartment in the up-and-coming area of South Boston, where he lived with his girlfriend, Sandra Gray. Outwardly, he appeared a perfectly average guy of medium height and build, with short fair hair and well presented. Yet he had a secret, an addiction to gambling, and was now in debt to the casino for $20,000. He couldn't pay. They had kept giving him credit, and as addicts do, he kept accepting it in the vein hope that he would have a good night on the tables and settle the debt. He never did.

On one particular night, he had been working the tables for a couple of hours and was losing badly. As the wheel spun, for what seemed like an eternity, he looked on anxiously for the ball to land on twenty-seven red, it ended up on fifteen black. He had reached the end of his credit. He knew he was in trouble, and he was not wrong. As he got up to leave the table, he felt a firm grip on his shoulder. Ryan looked round to see a giant of a man towering above him.

'Mr Martinez would like a word,' said the man, gruffly.

Ryan had no spit; he could not have spoken even if he'd wanted to. He simply nodded, resignedly. The man walked him slowly to an elevator that led to the office of Hugo Martinez. During the upward journey to the second floor, neither of the men spoke. The big man casually looked at his watch, somehow, it made Ryan feel uncomfortable. After which seemed a long time, the elevator came to a halt and the doors opened, leading straight into a spacious, luxurious office.

Martinez occasionally mingled with his clients in the casino, so Ryan recognised him immediately. A man of obvious Latin-American origin, he was in his forties, with straight, shoulder length black hair, parted in the middle. He stood 5' 11" tall with a pitted face and wore an elegant, tailored dinner suit. He was sitting behind an ornate antique desk and he smiled widely at Ryan as he entered.

'Please, come in and take a seat Mr Ryan,' Martinez said, gesturing to a single chair in front of his desk. He was smoking a very good Cuban cigar. The décor and fittings looked expensive, yet garish, from the wall coverings to his marble-topped desk. The one tasteful item was the deep piled cream carpet.

Ryan nervously sat down. 'Thank you,' were the only words he could find.

'I have some quite excellent brandy; would you care for some?' said Martinez gleefully.

'Uh, yes, thank you Mr Martinez,' Ryan replied nervously. Normally he wouldn't touch the stuff, he didn't like it, but if it soothed his nerves, why not.

Martinez got up and went to his drinks cabinet and poured out two large Brandies, while the big man, his all-round heavy, stood at the elevator entrance. Martinez returned to his desk, handing Ryan his glass before taking his seat once again.

His face took on a more serious appearance. 'Drink up, Mr Ryan. Here's to the future.' David Ryan tried to smile but couldn't, instead he took a small sip of the brandy.

'Well tell me, how is life treating you, Mr Ryan?' said Martinez.

'Could be better, I guess,' said Ryan with a nervous smile.

'Oh, I'm sorry to hear that. And how is your girlfriend – Sandra, isn't it?'

Ryan looked at Martinez in shock. 'She's fine.'

'I'm glad to hear that. And your job?'

'Fine, thank you.' The line of questioning was making him anxious.

'That's good, that's very good,' said Martinez. 'Well now, I think it's time we got down to business, don't you?'

Ryan knew this day was coming, but he had put it firmly to the back of his mind. Now it had arrived. 'I can pay you back all the money you've given me on credit, it may take a while, but I can do it in instalments. All I need is a little time, that's all,' said Ryan.

'Really?' said Martinez.

'Yes, I mean it might take me a year, but…'

Martinez shook his head. 'No, no, my friend, I'm afraid that simply won't do. You see, I don't run a charity, Mr Ryan, I run a business. I'm afraid if you can't pay your debt, well…'

'What? What are you going to do to me?'

'Oh, don't worry, Mr Ryan, we're not going to do anything to you. Your girlfriend, on the other hand…'

'Please, don't do anything to her. She's done nothing.'

'That entirely depends on your co-operation.'

'Co-operation?'

'Yes, Mr Ryan, that's correct – co-operation.'

'So what do you want from me? I've already told you I can't pay the money back straight away. If only you'd give me a little time – that's all I ask.'

'Forgive me, my friend, but you're in no position to ask for anything. I am however, in a position to ask a little favour from *you*. If you agree, then nothing will happen to you or your girlfriend and I can wipe your slate clean – how does that sound?'

'A favour? I don't know. What sort of favour?'

'Well, let's just say I have other business interests apart from this casino. I may need to call on you for assistance from time to time in your capacity as a customs officer. What do you say?'

'I'm not sure I know what you mean.'

'It's really quite simple Mr Ryan, I just want you to turn a blind-eye to, well, certain activities shall we say, involving my yacht in the harbour. What I mean exactly is this, you make sure she is not searched and is given clearance to come and go as she pleases, do you understand now?'

'Yes, I think I do,' said Ryan.

'Excellent!'

'You want me to break the law and risk losing my job, that's what you're asking.'

'Losing your job Mr Ryan wouldn't please me at all. It'd be entirely up to you to make sure that didn't happen. You see, if you did, you'd be of no use to me, and, well…'

From somewhere, Ryan found courage. 'And what if I went to the police and told them about this little chat?' he said.

'You and I know you're not going to do that Mr Ryan, don't we?'

'Are you willing to take that chance?' said Ryan.

'Yes, you know what, I think I am. You see, firstly, you have no proof of this conversation ever taking place. Secondly, I have a good many friends in the police. The commissioner himself in fact is a very dear friend. Ask yourself this, who do you think they would believe, a respectable businessman, or yourself. And then of course there's your girlfriend, Mr Ryan. No, you won't go to the police my friend.'

Ryan looked dejected and beaten. 'What do you want me to do exactly?'

'Don't worry about that now, I'll be in touch when I need you, but please, finish your brandy.'

Ryan took a large swallow, the liquor caught the back of his throat and made him cough. He caught his breath and spoke again. 'And when can I expect to hear from you?'

'Soon! don't look so worried Mr Ryan, it'll only be once, maybe twice a year that I'll call on you. Now that's not too much to ask for the amount of money you owe me, is it? or maybe I should say, owed me. And now we're friends, I shall call you David.'

'It's late, can I go now?'

'Of course. You're free to leave whenever you please.'

Ryan got up from the leatherbound chair and silently walked to the elevator door, Martinez bodyguard still stood there, muscular arms folded. The man pressed the button to open the door and Ryan stepped inside. Before the doors closed, Martinez called to him. 'Don't forget, David, we're partners now.'

Ryan said nothing in reply. The door closed and he descended with the bodyguard standing silently next to him. The casino was still busy as the door opened on the ground floor with Ryan stepping out of the elevator. The huge man escorted him from the premises and once outside, said, 'Don't forget Mr Ryan, we'll be watching you closely.'

'Yes, I'm sure of it,' he said, then hurried off to his car. He sat inside for several minutes, gathering his thoughts. He felt nauseous, physically shaken by the events of the evening. He knew he had no choice but to do as instructed and to keep his mouth firmly shut. He couldn't even tell his girlfriend. How could he even begin to explain to her, she didn't even know he gambled. As far as she was aware, his Saturday evenings out were spent with a group of his male buddies. Sandra was very comfortable with the idea of him spending some of his week-end with friends, he worked hard and deserved it, yet Ryan couldn't help feeling that if she ever found out the truth about his gambling addiction, it would most likely spell the end of their relationship.

Ryan, being an intelligent man, knew that Martinez operation must involve smuggling something in, or out of Boston, but what? He desperately needed to know what he was involved in and he aimed to find out. He drove to his home in South Boston, his mind in a whirl and arrived thirty-minutes later. He took a deep breath before entering his apartment. Sandra was curled up on the sofa watching an old romantic movie on the television, drinking a glass of wine.

'Hi Hun,' she said, as he entered the room, 'Good night out?'

He hesitated. 'Yeah, great, thanks.'

'How are the boys?'

'Oh yeah, they're all good.'

'Where'd you go?'

'Oh, you know, the usual, O'Malley's Bar. Shot some pool and the guys had a few too many beers. The usual Saturday night out.'

'And you, you poor thing, as the designated driver, you don't get to have a drink,' she said, getting up to kiss him. 'Although, I do smell something on your breath.'

'Uh, well, I did have one drink just for a change.'

'Well, one can't hurt, can it?' she said, smiling.

'That's what I thought,' he said, giving her a peck on the cheek. 'I think I'll have a beer now as a matter of fact – how's your wine?'

'No more for me, thanks, I'm fine.' She curled up on the sofa again.

At that moment, his cell phone rang, he did not recognise the number. 'I'll take this in the kitchen while I'm getting a beer.' He spoke in a hushed voice. 'Hello, who's this?'

'David, how is your lovely girlfriend?'

'Martinez?'

'That's right, David. I'm just calling to remind you of our conversation this evening.'

'Don't worry, I haven't forgotten. How could I?'

'And also, David, make sure you are on duty on Monday evening at 7pm. Is that clear?'

'But…'

'Just be there.' With that, Martinez hung up.

Chapter Two

Six Months Later - Present Day

It was the fourth time in six months that Martinez had contacted Ryan to make sure he was on duty on a particular day and at a specific time. It was invariably at night, and Ryan's requests for swapping shifts were, he thought, beginning to look suspicious. So much for once or twice a year. Yet it seemed he was powerless to change the situation. Yes, in some ways he had brought it on himself, he was painfully aware of that, but he also suspected that Martinez had allowed him to get into debt deliberately, he had fallen firmly into a trap.

It was exactly 11pm on a Sunday night when Ryan got the call from Martinez.

'David, I take it you're on duty as I asked?' said Martinez.

'Yes, I'm on duty, but it's becoming difficult – these constant shift changes…'

'Don't worry so much, David. Everything will be just fine. Just leave the worrying to me, okay, my friend?'

'Yeah, well that's easy for you to say. They'll throw away the key if I get caught. I don't even know what it is you're dealing in – is it drugs?'

Martinez took on a more serious tone. 'That doesn't concern you.'

'But it does concern me, I think I've paid my debt to you, I don't want to do this anymore.'

'Oh, you don't want to do it anymore! No, my friend, I haven't finished with you yet. Your debt is far from repaid, for yours and your girlfriend's sake, please don't think otherwise. Now, my yacht will be coming into the harbour at midnight – make sure you're there to greet her as usual.'

'But I…'

'Adios, David,' said Martinez, before hanging up. He reclined in the oxblood leather chair at his desk with a worried look on his face. 'Our boy is beginning to concern me,' he said to his two heavies, he took a deep lungful of cigar smoke and blew it out in a cloud that almost obscured him to the others for a moment. 'Bobby, I think you'd better get down to the harbour – keep an eye on him. But be discreet, okay.'

'Yes boss.' Unquestioning, the man left the office, and as it was a Sunday, strolled through the eerily empty casino and out to his car. He drove straight to the harbour.

Ryan stood at the waterfront waiting, the evening was warm and calm, the waves gently striking the harbour wall. The many floodlights bathed the harbour, but not this particular mooring. Martinez had planned his operation well and had paid for one of the few dimly lit areas to moor his yacht, it was ideal. Ryan was feeling tense, knowing very well that he could not continue doing this, yet the consequences of stopping working for Martinez were unthinkable.

He had thought long and hard about coming clean with Sandra. Admitting to her his gambling problem and about Martinez blackmailing him. He had also considered the possibility of the two of them moving far away, but didn't think Sandra would agree because of her career at The Bostonian Bank in the financial district. Besides, would it do any good? he thought, Martinez would find them and wreak revenge as he had promised, wherever they went, people like him would always find you.

Ryan had a good relationship with Sandra, he loved her very much. She was an understanding woman, fair-minded and intelligent, yet he wondered how she would be able to forgive the fact he had been living a lie all this time. Maybe, he thought, it would be fairer to tell her the truth, once and for all, and allow her to decide for herself what to do. She deserved better than this, he thought. His main concern though, was her safety and wondered if it would be best if she were to leave him and make a fresh start.

It was 12.10am when the Martinez yacht, its engine chugging at low speed, came in to its mooring. Ryan looked on anxiously as he had on the previous occasions. This was the fourth time in six months. Martinez had promised it would only happen a couple of times a year, and it was beginning to take a toll on his nerves. As always, the crew of the yacht got to work immediately, as Ryan, for the sake of appearances, boarded the vessel.

The crew, a mean looking bunch, arrogantly ignored his presence while they unloaded their cargo of six boxes. A van waited close by for the transfer to take place with two rough looking characters. They wasted no time, they loaded the containers into the back of the van and as always, simultaneously handed three holdalls to the yachts crew which they hurriedly stashed away. The whole operation took minutes, the van drove off and the yacht got underway once again.

During the operation, Martinez's man, Bobby, had been observing the exchange through night-vision binoculars from a safe distance. He took out his cell phone and reported back to Martinez.

'It all went smoothly boss; our stooge did his job, good as gold.'

'Excellent,' said Martinez, 'you may as well go home now, Bobby.' He put his feet up on his desk and smiled to himself, while drinking a brandy and smoking a cigar. He felt his operation could not fail with Ryan in his grasp, he had no intention of releasing that grasp at any time in the near future.

After his shift had ended, Ryan went home, it was 8am and Sandra had already left for the city. It had seemed a long night, yet he couldn't contemplate going to bed, his mind was spinning, his stomach churning too much for sleep. He had no idea what the packages were going out of Boston, yet it was a fair bet that the ones coming in were drugs of some kind – cocaine was his best guess. He wanted no further part in it.

Despite the early hour, he poured himself a glass of Jamesons. He took several deep swallows of the liquor and lit a cigarette, he only smoked when he was feeling particularly tense, and this, without doubt, was one of those occasions. It was not until 11am that he finally found the courage to phone Martinez on his personal line.

'Good morning,' said Martinez, cheerfully.

'Martinez, it's David Ryan.'

'David, how nice to hear from you. I hear you did a good job last night.'

'Never mind that, I'm phoning to tell you I don't want any more part in your little caper. I'm done!'

'I see,' Martinez said, more seriously, 'well, I'm sorry to hear you say that, David. Perhaps a little reminder of what I'm capable of is in order. How *is* your lovely girlfriend, by the way?'

'I'm not taking your threats anymore. If you so much as touch her, I swear to God, I'll tell the police everything, even if it means I go to jail.'

'That would be most unwise my friend,' said Martinez.

'Unwise or not, I swear I'll do it, unless you promise to stay away from her.'

'I see – most unfortunate.' Martinez left the words hanging and put the receiver down.

'What was that all about, boss?' asked one of his men.

'That was Ryan. It seems he doesn't want to play anymore. He's threatening me, Me! With the police,' he said furiously.

'What you gonna do?' said Bobby.

'I don't think we have any choice in the matter, do you. Take care of it, Bobby. But do it quietly, okay.'

Bobby nodded in acknowledgement.

'Trouble, baby?' asked one of Martinez's girlfriends, getting up from a plush sofa and caressing him.

'Nothing that can't be dealt with,' he said, pushing her away.

Ryan was thinking clearly now, he knew what he had to do. He dialled Sandra's office number, then, when prompted, tapped in her personal extension. He took another swallow of Jamesons before she answered.

'Sandra Gray, speaking.'

'Hi, Honey, it's David.'

'David, what's up? I thought you would be in bed.'

'I couldn't sleep.'

'Is something wrong?'

'Yes, Honey, I'm afraid there is.'

'Well, what is it, David?'

'Now, listen to me carefully, Honey,' he hesitated before continuing, 'I don't quite know how to say this…'

'David, you're scaring me – what's wrong?'

'I can't explain everything now, I'm not sure I ever can, but I'm in trouble, Sandy.'

'Trouble? What sort of trouble?'

'Listen carefully. When you come home, I want you to pack a few things and go stay with your mother for a few days.'

'Now you're really beginning to scare me. Can't you tell me what this is all about?'

'No, not over the phone. Just do as I ask. I love you, Sandy.'

'You have to tell me something, David.'

'I can't.'

'But you must, if it's that bad…'

'I told you, I can't explain over the phone – it's too complicated. Just phone your mother to say you'll be staying with her for a few days, that's all I ask. I love you.' Ryan hung up and lit another cigarette. His finger hovered over the keypad of his cell-phone, he desperately wanted this thing to end, and calling the police seemed almost the only way. But then he remembered Martinez's words, saying that he was a personal friend of the police commissioner and others within the police department.

Were it so, would the police believe his story? And even if they did, would they be in the pocket of Martinez so much as to simply turn a blind-eye? If all this was the case, then it could be him going to jail, not Martinez. He had heard horror stories about what life was like in a correctional facility, he wasn't sure he could survive it. Ryan threw his phone down on the kitchen worktop. He paced the floor, taking frequent swallows of his Jamesons, his head was beginning to pound. He locked up the apartment and went for a walk and to get some air.

Chapter Three

Ryan walked long into the afternoon in a kind of daze. He had crossed Congress Street Bridge and found himself at O'Mally's bar near the waterfront. It was around 3.30pm, he went inside the bar and ordered a beer, the place was virtually empty. He knew the barman well.

'So, what brings you here at this time of the day?' said the barman, placing the beer on the counter.

'I just wanted a beer – if that's okay with you?' Ryan, said sullenly.

'Hey, man, don't get me wrong, it's pretty quiet and I'm glad of the company, it's just that…'

'Yeah, well, I don't think I'd be very good company at the moment.'

'Something wrong, man? Do you want to talk?'

'No, I don't. In fact, I think I'll just take my beer and sit quietly in the corner.' Ryan said, raising himself from the bar-stool.

He found a table and sat down, alone with his thoughts. He no longer cared about himself; his thoughts surrounded Sandra. They had lived together for over a year and his life had come to revolve around her. Yet he had lied to her time and time again about his gambling habit, and more recently, about the impossible situation he had found himself in. She deserved better, he thought, at the very least, she deserved the truth.

How would he do it? How could he begin to explain his lies? Would she be understanding or would she leave him? He couldn't blame her if she did leave him, in fact, maybe she would be better off without him, he thought. His only concern now was her safety. He looked solemnly to the bottom of his empty beer glass and signalled to the barman for another of the same.

The smartly dressed barman duly arrived at his table with another beer. He laid it on the table and paused for a moment. Then he grabbed a chair and sat down, squarely facing Ryan.

'Look man, I've seen it all in this job, and I know when someone's in trouble. Now, you can tell me to mind my own business if you like, but I'm your friend, so why don't you talk to me about it? – whatever it is.'

'I know you're only trying to help, Pete, but you're right, it's none of your goddammed business, so why don't you just leave me alone,' he said, in uncharacteristic fit of temper.

The barman looked shocked. 'Okay, man, okay, if that's the way you want it, that's how it'll be. Enjoy your beer and I hope you get it sorted, whatever it is.'

A customer shouted impatiently over to Pete from the bar.

'Yeah, yeah, I'm coming,' he shouted back. Turning to Ryan, he simply said, 'good-luck. See you around, man.'

'Just one thing,' said Ryan, 'bring me another beer when you get a moment.'

The barman looked thoughtfully at him for a moment. 'You planning on getting drunk? Sure, if that's what you really want?'

'Yeah, it's what I want,' said Ryan.

The afternoon had passed without Ryan noticing. He glanced at his watch; his vision slightly blurred from too many beers. It was 5.30pm and he suddenly realised that Sandra would shortly be arriving back at their apartment. He knew he couldn't face her in person and being partially drunk wouldn't make matters any better. He decided to wait a short time and then call her. But he didn't have to wait, at 5.45pm, she called him. He hesitated before answering.

'David, where are you? I've been worried sick,' said Sandra.

'I'm so sorry, Honey, I just couldn't face you. I know I'm a coward, but…'

'Just tell me what the hell's going on, David?'

'It's a long story, Honey.'

'Well! I'm listening.'

'The truth is, Sandy, my life has been one big lie. You see, I have a problem, it's a problem I've had since before we even met.'

'What sort of problem, tell me for God's sake.'

'Gambling, it's gambling.'

'I see,' said Sandra, in a dismayed tone, 'but what has that to do with you telling me to move to my mother's? There must be more to it than that.'

'I'm afraid there is. These people kept giving me credit until I was in debt to them for twenty-thousand-dollars.'

'Twenty-thousand? Are you mad, David?'

'I'm afraid there's more. They got me in debt to them deliberately, they must have done checks on me, found out what my job was, and blackmailed me into helping them in an illegal business.'

'What sort of illegal business?'

'I'm not even sure myself, but I think it may be drug smuggling. I had to make sure their yacht had safe passage through the harbour. But I told the boss of the organisation today, that I'm having nothing more to do with it. That's why you have to leave – tonight. He's made threats. You must go to your mother's now.'

'Oh David, why didn't you tell me the truth about the gambling, I would have got you help, but now it's one big mess.'

'Sandy, I don't expect you to forgive me, find someone new, someone that's worth being with, because I'm not worth it.'

'Oh David.'

'Just promise me, you'll pack some things right now and get out of there. Will you do that for me?'

'Okay, if you really think it's necessary. But what about my job?'

'Just tell your office that you're sick or something, it'll only be for a few days.'

'And what about you?'

'I'll be okay, don't worry. I'm going to the police; I'm going to tell them everything.'

19

'Just be careful, David.'

'So, you're going to leave now, right?'

'Yes, I suppose so. When will I see you?'

'As soon as it's safe, that is, if you want to see me again. I won't blame you if you never want to see me again.'

'Well, we certainly have a lot to discuss, but yes, of course I do. We can get through this.'

'I'll call you, Honey. Goodbye,' said David.

Ryan felt a degree of relief that the truth was finally out, it had been a burden he had carried for the year that Sandra and he had lived together. He was also relieved in the knowledge she had taken him seriously about going to stay with her mother for a few days. Yet, right now, he had no desire to go home to his apartment. He decided to stay at the bar for another few drinks and maybe a bite to eat.

His head suddenly felt clearer now, he knew exactly what he had to do. He decided that the next day he would go to the police precinct and tell them everything, even if he himself were arrested for aiding criminals. As for Martinez having friends in high places within the Boston police department, he would cross that bridge when he came to it, he thought. All he knew was, he wanted a fresh start, including, as Sandra had suggested, seeking help for his gambling addiction.

Pete, the barman was changing shift with a couple of evening staff. From around 7pm, the bar would usually get much busier and with live music, had a good atmosphere. Pete made a point of passing by Ryan's table. He stopped briefly to speak to him.

'How you doing, man?'

'I'm fine, Pete. Look, man, I'm sorry I snapped at you earlier, I had things on my mind.'

'Forget it. You okay now?'

'Yeah, I'm feeling much better, thanks.'

'Good! But listen, you've had a lot of booze, why don't you call it a day and go home.'

'Yeah, I think I will, I'll have something to eat, then go home.'

'Okay, buddy, you take care and I'll see you around.'

'Yeah, see you around, Pete.'

By 10pm, Ryan had still not eaten and was still drinking. The place by now was buzzing with customers and live Irish folk music. It was around this time that Frank Doyle entered the spacious bar. With tables dotted around, it was one of his favourite bars. He made brief eye-contact with Ryan as he strolled past his table, and headed towards the bar.

'Evening, Danny,' Frank said to the barman, as he scoured the place for a free table. It had low, atmospheric lighting, but he spotted a table that was free, ordered a beer and one of their special burgers with fries.

'I'll bring the food over to you when it's ready, Frank,' said Danny.

'Thanks, Danny,' Frank replied. He took his beer and seated himself at his chosen table. He'd had another long day working on two cases simultaneously. Affairs of matrimony were his bread and butter, even if they could become monotonous. But business had been good for his one-man private investigation company since he had moved to Boston – he was not complaining.

Being an ex-cop from NYPD homicide, he had certainly had his share of excitement, enough to last a lifetime in fact. Being shot at several times in a career was quite enough for anyone. But then, he'd had a couple of out of the ordinary cases in his capacity as a private investigator as well. On one occasion he had been stabbed, yes, routine work suited him just fine.

About ten minutes later, Danny arrived at his table with the food he had ordered. Burgers, fries, hotdogs, these were the types of food which made up Frank's staple diet, he also enjoyed a beer or two and smoked too many cigars. He was still overweight and he knew it.

'So, how are things, Frank? Haven't seen you for a while,' said Danny.

'Good, never been busier. How about you?'

'Can't complain, Frank. What good would it do anyway,' he laughed.

'Yeah, that's true enough,' said Frank, chuckling.

'You see that guy over there?' he discreetly indicated Ryan's table, 'Now there's a guy with problems if ever I saw one. Been here virtually all afternoon according to Pete.'

'You know him?' asked Frank.

'Yeah, he comes in pretty often with friends or his girl. Never seen him like this though, laid-back type of guy usually. Anyway, I'd better get back, enjoy, Frank.'

At about 11pm, Ryan decided he'd had enough to drink and would take the long walk back to his apartment. He got unsteadily to his feet, paid his tab and left. Frank finished his second beer some ten minutes later and also decided it was time to go home for some much-needed sleep. He went over to the bar, paid and said goodnight to Danny before leaving.

Frank, once outside, lit a cigar and inhaled its deliciousness in. He started to walk to his car, but thought he heard something coming from an alleyway next to O'Malley's. He wasn't carrying his gun, he rarely did. He cautiously entered the alley to investigate. It was dimly lit, but he followed the sound, it was a person, and by the sound of it, that person was in trouble.

He could just make out that it was the same person who Danny had pointed out to him in the bar. The man was badly wounded, blood spurted from his neck. Frank took a handkerchief from his pocket and applied pressure to the wound. He had seen such wounds before and knew that the man would be gone by the time an ambulance arrived.

Frank put his ear closer to the man's mouth as he tried to speak.

'Marteee... Marteeen…' the words would not come as he coughed up blood.

'Martin? Martin who?' asked Frank.

But it was no use, he couldn't speak anymore. Ryan died in Frank's arms.

Chapter Four

Frank lowered Ryan's head gently to the ground, dialled 911 on his cell phone and requested police and ambulance. Whoever had done this, had long gone, there was no sign of anyone in the vicinity. Yet, it could only have happened in the last few minutes, Frank had left the bar just minutes after Ryan.

Frank carefully took out Ryan's wallet from his jacket pocket. He looked inside and found that the man's credit cards and cash were still there, it ruled out the possibility of a mugging, in any case, this particular area of Boston was not known for muggings, in fact it had a low crime rate generally. After examining Ryan's work ID card and driver's license, he made a mental note of the name and address and replaced the wallet.

He remembered the words of Danny. The man he had now identified as David Ryan clearly had problems. His heavy prolonged drinking, it seemed, was uncharacteristic of the man. Did this have anything to do with his murder? Frank wondered. Frank was sure of one thing, this was no random killing, someone, it seemed, wanted the man dead.

Minutes later, an ambulance arrived at the scene, followed quickly by a police patrol car, plus two unmarked police vehicles, their sirens wailing. The commotion attracted some interest with a number of customers from the bar coming outside to see what was happening, their number included Danny. Frank stood back to let the ambulance staff and police do their work. The paramedics pronounced Ryan dead and allowed the police to examine the body. A call went out from the lieutenant for a forensics team to be called to the scene.

In all the confusion, Danny found Frank standing back from the scene. 'What's going on, Frank?' he asked.

'That guy you pointed out to me inside – he's in that side street. Looks like he's been murdered. I must've just missed it.'

'Woh, David? Murdered? Jesus, Hey, do you think it's got anything to do with the mood he was in, Frank?'

'I'd put real money on it,' said Frank. 'How well did you know him?'

'Uh, well, Pete knew him better than me. But I knew him enough to say he was carrying a load on his shoulders today, that's for sure.'

'Hey, Frank!' came the familiar voice of Detective John McKay from the crowd gathered outside O'Malley's.

'John, I didn't see you there, how you doing?' said Frank.

'Yeah, fine Frank. dispatch gave your name as the one who put the call in, is that right?'

'Yeah, that's right. I found him. You assigned to this case?'

'Along with the boss,' he said, shrugging, with a look of contempt.

'Was he dead when you found him, Frank?' asked McKay.

'No, but he only lasted about a minute. He was drowning in his own blood. He tried to talk, sounded like he was trying to say something like, Martin or Marty, that's all he said. This is no random killing is it, John?'

'What makes you say that, Frank?' he said, noting the name, Martin, that Frank had given him in his notebook.

'Well, he wasn't robbed,' said Frank.

'Yeah, we figured that out. Hold on! How did you know that? Don't tell me, you went through his pockets, Frank.'

'Well, maybe just a little.'

'Jesus Frank, whatever you do, don't let the lieutenant find out or he'll likely arrest you for interfering with evidence. Who's this guy anyway?' he asked, gesturing towards Danny.

'This is Danny Pearce; he works in O'Malley's. You may want to talk to him, the dead man apparently spent most of the day in the bar.'

'Okay Frank, thanks for your help, I'll pass the info onto the lieutenant. Now, take my advice, buddy – go home and leave it to us, okay. We'll need a statement of course.'

'You've got it.'

'We'll get together for a drink some time, Frank, okay.'

'Sure thing, John. Goodnight.'

Frank returned to his car and immediately took out his notebook from the glovebox. He quickly jotted down from memory the name of the victim, his address and the place where he worked. Also, the name Ryan had tried to tell him. Yet, Frank wondered if it was the name of a person at all. It could mean anything, he thought, the name of a person *or* a place. It was not much to go on.

In any case, he thought, it was nothing to do with him, John McKay was right, it was a police matter, not that of a private investigator. He took the fifteen-minute drive home, took a shower, scrubbing his hands to remove the traces of dried blood and went to bed with his thoughts.

Over the next three days, Frank's time was spent either in his car or on foot following a suspected unfaithful husband and likewise a wife that was also suspected of the same. He used his time equally on each case. There was nothing to suggest any infidelity in either case so far and he reported as much to his clients. The client of the husband was satisfied and stopped the investigation, paying Frank what she owed him. The other client wanted Frank to continue tailing his wife as he still believed adamantly that she was having an affair.

It was the man's prerogative; it would pay a few bills.

He said he would continue the surveillance and the next day, after following the woman, Frank sat in his car while she entered a restaurant, he took photographs of her entering the building and noted the time and date. Then, after a few minutes had passed, he entered the restaurant in the guise of a customer requiring a table. As he waited for an attendant, he glanced around the place in search of the woman. It was busy, but he eventually spotted her sitting at a table with what was obviously a female friend. With nothing to report there, he left hurriedly and returned to his car.

This alone, of course, did not prove her innocence, it was often the case that the suspected wife or husband went on somewhere else, so to be certain, he waited in the car again until she would appear from the restaurant. Frank took his newspaper which he had so far not had a chance to read. As he read on, buried in the paper was just a few lines about Ryan's murder.

"David Ryan, 35(Pictured) was found brutally murdered on 22nd March in The Waterfront area of Boston. A police spokesperson said it was a tragic waste of life and the police were treating it as what appeared to be a random killing without motive."

Frank could not believe what he was reading. He dialled the number for Boston PD homicide.

It rang only a couple of times before someone answered. 'Homicide.'

'Yeah, is John McKay on duty today?'

'He's out of the office, Buddy, can I help?'

'No – it's okay, I'll try again later.'

'Please yourself, Buddy,' said the detective, before hanging up abruptly.

Frank was still astounded. What kind of investigation *was* this? He wondered.

There was nothing he could do, at least not until his working day was through. He still had the woman in the restaurant to concentrate on. He sat for an hour and thirty minutes before she finally emerged with her girlfriend at 2.45pm. Her clothes were clearly expensive, but they were also tacky. It didn't always follow that money gave a person good taste, he thought. They pecked one another on each cheek before going their separate ways. Frank snapped another photograph of the two women before they parted, believing it would satisfy the suspicious husband.

Her Mercedes convertible was parked right outside the restaurant, she drove off and Frank followed at a discreet distance. It soon became clear she was driving in the direction of her home in the affluent Seaport neighbourhood. He made sure by following until she pulled into the long driveway of the veritable mansion, then drove back to his office.

Once there, he took out a cold beer from the fridge in his office and poured it into a glass, he could not stand drinking a beer straight from the bottle. He picked up his office phone and dialled out the number for homicide again. He was in luck this time.

'Detective McKay, homicide.'

'John, it's Frank Doyle.'

'Oh, Hi Frank. What can I do you for?'

'What the hell's going on with that David Ryan case, John?'

'What do you mean?'

'You know what I mean, from what I read in the newspaper, the case is virtually closed.'

'Nah, it's still open, Frank. There's just not enough to go on at the moment, that's all there is to it.'

'We both know that was no random killing.'

'Look, Frank, I don't have to remind you, do I, you're no longer a cop, Buddy. Just let sleeping dogs lie okay, and let us do our job.'

'What's that supposed to mean? Something stinks, John.'

'Frank, I'll level with you,' McKay said, lowering his voice, 'we made enquiries, but the decision to pull the plug came from on-high, you get me? It's just not a priority at the moment.'

'Yeah, I get you, and it still stinks.'

'Look, Man, you're my friend, and my advice to you is forget it. You don't want to get involved, believe me, this is a police matter.'

'Maybe, maybe not. Just tell me who's behind pulling the plug?'

'You know I can't do that, Frank, and even if I could, I wouldn't because it's none of your goddamned business,' he said, raising his voice.

'You're right, I shouldn't have asked you. I guess I'll just have to find some answers myself.' Frank slowly put the receiver down, took a swallow of his beer and lit a cigar.

Chapter Five

Frank consulted the brief notes he had made after leaving the murder scene three days ago. If the police had little to go on, then he had virtually nothing, just Ryan's name, address, place of work and of course, the man's indistinct dying word, which sounded like – Martin or Marty. It was clearly the name of someone he knew. The murderer himself perhaps?

There were three messages on his answering machine, all potentially new matrimonial cases, he called the numbers back and requested that each of his potential clients visit him at his office to discuss their concerns at their convenience. He next read the mail which had come through his door earlier that day, there was nothing of importance, although there was a cheque from a client he had recently worked for and a couple of bills. He really should hire a secretary, he thought.

He glanced at the framed photograph of his late wife on his desk and wondered if he ever would have gone into private investigations had she still been here. She had passed away while he was still a serving cop in New York. He retired shortly after her death; he had a reasonable pension; they could have enjoyed retirement together so much. Yet once she had gone and he had retired from the NYPD, life seemed empty and pointless. That was when he decided to fill his time with his own agency in Maine.

It had been tough at first, business in Maine had not exactly been brisk. But since his move to Boston, the cases coming in had been almost continuous. Most of his work came by word-of-mouth, he had a good reputation and being an ex-cop helped. He had neither the time nor the inclination for romantic involvement, no one could replace his Marjy. He kissed her photo, 'Love you, Honey,' he said to her. He locked up the office and took the stairs to his apartment above to take a short nap.

His nap was longer than he had planned. He woke up with a start and looked at his watch, it was 5.30pm and he was hungry. He had only had a sandwich all day. He got up from the sofa wearily and made his way to the kitchen, made some coffee, and in an attempt to eat healthily, prepared a meal of salad and a little cold meat. All of this time, he could not stop thinking about the Ryan case and why it had been pulled. John McKay had said the decision had come from above. Who had decided to pull in the reigns, and why? These were the questions that bothered Frank.

John had been correct in saying it was a police matter, yet his attitude towards Frank, was one he had not seen before. Frank was certain the killing had not been random or a mugging gone wrong. There was something not right and it was his intention to find out more. There was one thing for sure, he could not work alongside the police on this, he was not even sure he could trust his friend, John McKay.

Frank decided he would start his investigation immediately, starting with a visit to Ryan's address. He hadn't a clue if the man was married or if he lived alone, but he hoped there would be someone who could at least answer some of his questions. He took a shower, changed his clothes and by 7pm was making his way to Ryan's apartment block in South Boston, hoping it would not be a wasted journey.

Forty-five minutes later, he arrived at Pine Grove Terrace, it looked to be a pleasant area. He parked his car and made his way through the revolving glass door of the apartment block and looked at the board stating the apartment numbers by floor. Number forty-two was on the fourth floor. There was an intercom system for each apartment, he pressed the appropriate button and waited. After a few moments, a voice came over the speaker, it was the voice of a woman and she sounded scared.

'Who is it?'

'Good-evening, Ma'am, my name is Frank Doyle, I'm a private investigator. I wondered if I could ask you a few questions?'

'Private investigator?'

'If it's inconvenient…'

'What do you want to know?'

'Uh, it's about David Ryan. Do you think I could come up?'

'I've already spoken to the police.'

'Yes, of course, but I'd like to ask you some questions myself. You see, I'm the one who found David.'

'How do I know you are who you say you are?'

'I have my ID, but if you prefer, you could come to my office. My address is in the phone book.'

'You sound genuine. You'd better come up.'

'Thanks Ma'am.'

Frank entered the elevator and within seconds was on the fourth floor. He found the apartment and rang the door-bell.

'I've had a camera installed, can you hold your ID up to it please,' said Sandra, nervously.

Frank did as she asked and then heard the door chain being released and the door opening. 'Thank you for seeing me,' he said, gently.

'I'm not sure I understand, Mr…'

'Doyle, but please, call me Frank.'

'Would you like some coffee, Mr Doyle? I was just about to make some.'

'Yes, That'd be great, thank you.'

'You say you were the one who found David?' she said, 'Did he suffer?'

'No, it was very quick,' Frank reassured her. 'May I ask you, are you his wife?'

'No, we lived together.'

'I'm sorry for your loss, Miss… I'm sorry, I don't know your name.'

'Gray, Sandra Gray. I still don't quite understand Mr Doyle, what's your interest in all of this?'

Frank answered her question, with a question. 'What did the police tell you about his murder, Sandra?'

Sandra began to weep a little. 'They told me it was a senseless random murder. That was all they could tell me. But I don't believe that for one moment, Mr Doyle.'

'What makes you say that?'

'He was in deep trouble, I knew nothing about it until the evening he died, we spoke on the phone and he told me he had a huge gambling debt. And he also told me he was being blackmailed into doing something illegal, I don't know what it was, but he said he was going to the police. He also said I was in danger and I should stay with my mother, which I did. I've only been back here a couple of days. I told the police all of this.'

'That's interesting. Well, that's why I'm here. I don't believe his murder was random either. Tell me, does the name Martin or Marty mean anything to you?'

'No, not at all. Why?'

'He was trying to tell me something, I'm not sure what.'

'I'll get that coffee,' said Sandra.

'Not on my account, please. I'll leave you in peace and here's my card. If you think of anything, don't hesitate to call me. Do you think I could take your number? That way, if I find out anything I can give you a call.'

Sandra gave Frank a card with her home and office number on it.

'So, you're going to make enquiries on your own – why?' she asked.

'Let's just say I like to see proper justice done. I was a homicide detective in the NYPD. I think there's something very wrong with this case. I'll be in touch, Miss Gray.'

'Thank you, Mr Doyle, if you do get to the bottom of this, I'll gladly pay you. It seems the police don't want to find out the truth, I'd be glad to have someone on David's side.'

'Oh, just one other thing. Would you have a photo of David I could borrow?'

'Yes, of course.' She rummaged through a drawer, found a photo album, and picked one out. 'Will this do?' she said.

'Yes, that'll do just fine, thanks. Well, goodbye, Ma'am, and once again, I'm very sorry.'

'Goodbye, Mr Doyle, and thank you.'

The door closed behind him and he heard the rattle of the door-chain being put back into place. Frank left in the certain knowledge that his instinct had been correct, there was much more to this case than even he had imagined. It still did not give him much to go on, but it was a start at least.

Frank knew of at least two illegal gambling holes in the district, and the people that ran them were unsavoury characters for sure. Perhaps, he thought, it would be a good idea to pay them a visit first. But that could wait until tomorrow. For now, he needed to process the information given to him by Ryan's girlfriend.

It had been a long day, Frank took the drive home, while all the time thinking about David Ryan's mysterious death. His dying words echoed in Frank's head – Martin – Marty.

Chapter Six

Frank's morning started out much like any other day, answering phone calls from present and prospective clients, printing out photographic evidence from his previous day's surveillance, and compiling reports. He then strolled down to the sandwich bar, a few doors down from his office, bought a bacon baguette and set off on another day of tracking the movements of the allegedly unfaithful wife.

He drove past the couple's mansion and noted that the woman's car was still in the driveway, he parked a discreet distance away and waited for any movement. Thirty-minutes went by and at last, his rear-view mirror, he saw her car pull out of the driveway and heading South. He turned his car around and followed as closely as he could.

This time, the journey was much longer than the previous day. It took Frank on a forty-minute drive out of town until she eventually pulled into a motel. This looked dubious. Perhaps the husband's suspicions were correct after all, Frank thought. As she got out of her car, Frank took a photograph and noted the time. Then all he could do was wait again. It was a long wait. Two hours later, she emerged from the motel with a man, he looked a giant of a man, dressed in a dark suit, a white shirt opened almost to his chest and black patent leather shoes that you could have seen your face in. A gold chain hung from his neck. Frank zoomed in and took another series of photographs as they kissed one another on the lips and parted company.

The only thing left for Frank to do was produce the evidence, what the luckless husband did after that was in his hands. Frank, though, suspected he would be called to give evidence at some point in the future, in a costly divorce trial. Case well and truly closed he thought, and drove back to his office.

Yet in all of this time, his mind was on the Ryan case. He had so little information to work on, he was not sure what to do next other than visiting the gambling holes, as he had previously considered. It was the only option open to him at the moment, and so he decided they would be his first line of enquiry. He diverted to Roxbury.

Roxbury was one of the most rundown and dangerous districts in Boston. Most people, including the police, knew of the illegal gambling that went on, yet they turned a blind-eye, crime was rife, it was virtually a no-go area. At least it was daytime, no one, except those looking for a game of poker would set foot in the area at night. Frank knew a guy who ran one of the joints and that's where he started.

Frank parked his car outside the place, hoping it would still be there when he came out. He entered the grimy place which was disguised as nothing but a bar, the games took place in a back room and the stakes were usually high. The bar was poorly lit, the air full of stale cigarette smoke. There were only a few guys standing around drinking, two others played pool. They all stopped what they were doing and stared at Frank as he walked in. It was unnerving even for a hardened ex-cop from New York.

The two rough looking tattooed men playing pool, stopped their game and played menacingly with their pool cues as he walked past them to the bar.

The bartender looked blankly at him and said nothing. 'Give me a beer,' Frank said, showing no sign of fear or weakness. He lit a cigar. The weedy looking bartender scowled, but pulled a bottle from the cooler and placed it sharply on the counter.

'That'll be four bucks.'

'Got a beer glass?' said Frank assertively.

The scruffy man, tried to stare Frank out for a few moments, then got a glass and thumped it to the counter.

'Sam around?' asked Frank, placing five dollars down on the counter.

'Who's asking?'

'Just tell him it's Frank Doyle.'

'Wait there,' said the man, coming out from behind the bar. He went to a door on the opposite side of the room, knocked and entered. After a minute, the bartender emerged with Sam.

'Hey, Frankie, what brings you to this part of town?' he shouted across the bar in an attempt to look pleased to see him. Sam was never pleased to see anyone but punters looking for a game.

'Wondered if I could have a word, Sam.'

The man's face took on a more serious appearance. 'Sure, step into my office.'

Frank entered the grimy room that Sam called his office. 'You carrying, Frankie?'

Frank shook his head, but lifted his arms anyway. He knew he would be frisked.

'Good enough, Frankie, I trust you. Okay, Rob, you can leave us now.' The bartender left them alone and returned to his work. 'So, what can I do for you, Frankie?'

Frank reached for the photo in his breast pocket and placed it on Sam's desk. 'Have you seen this guy before?'

Sam picked up the picture and studied it. He hesitated. 'What's it to you, Frankie?'

'The poor guy's dead – take another look, Sam.'

Sam rubbed his stubbled chin. 'He may have been in a couple of times. People come and go; you know how it is.'

'Yeah, I know how it is. But you think you've seen him here?'

'I guess so. You're not trying to pin anything on me now, are you Frankie?'

'Relax, I'm not trying to pin anything on anybody. Just tell me, did he owe you money?'

'Now look, Frank…'

'Come on, Sam, we both know what you're running here. Just tell me one thing – did he owe you any money?'

'No, of course not. We don't run credit here. You can either pay your way or you can't. if you can't, you're out of the game – simple as that. What happened to the guy anyway?'

'He was murdered. And he owed someone a lot of money.'

'Well, it wouldn't be any of the joints around here, none of us do credit.'

'Okay Sam, thanks for your help anyway.'

'Anytime, Frankie,' said Sam, seeing Frank off the premises. 'Hey listen, have you thought of Hugo's Casino? They give credit.'

'Pretty unlikely they'd be involved, they're a respectable joint as far as I know – no offence, Sam.'

'Huh, I don't know about that. I hear Hugo's a pretty nasty piece of work.'

'Well, maybe I'll look in sometime – check it out.'

'Just be careful, Frankie, that's all.'

'Thanks for the advice. See you around, Sam.'

Frank left Sam and went outside, the sun dazzled him after the dim lighting of the bar. He was relieved to find his car intact. There were plenty of youths that should have been in school patrolling the streets looking for trouble. He drove out of the area as quickly as he could and headed for his office.

Frank made himself a coffee and set to work on his matrimonial case. He typed his report out on his computer, printed it, then called the husband, a Mr Robinson, on his personal cell phone to break the news of his wife's certain infidelity. He did not have the identity of the man as yet, but the length of stay in the motel along with the photographic evidence was more than enough to show she was being unfaithful. Frank suggested that the husband visit him at his office where he could hand him the evidence.

The man was inconsolable at first, yet it quickly turned to rage. Frank had seen it a thousand times before. There were no winners in this game. The man agreed to come to his office the next morning. Frank made himself another coffee and leaned back in his chair, pondering the Ryan case and what Sam had told him about the casino boss. Sam may have been many things, but he had proved himself a reliable source in the past. And if as he said, Hugo was a nasty character, that was good enough for him to investigate further.

Frank sat upright, and amid the mad world that it was, he picked up the phone to call his daughter and regain, if only for a few minutes, some normality in his life.

'Hi Mary, it's Dad. Just thought I'd give you a call to see how you and the kids are.'

'Hi Dad, yes, we're all fine. How are you? Haven't heard from you for a few days, what are you doing?'

'Oh, nothing much, the usual, you know.'

'How about you?'

'The same old routine, nothing to report, but it's all good. You should come over for lunch some time, how about Sunday?'

'Yes, maybe, I'll let you know for certain if I can make it or not. Things are a little busy at the moment, but I'll try.'

'You could bring your friend if you like.'

'Friend?'

'Laura, of course.'

'Oh, I'm sure she'll have something of her own on. I'll let you know, sweetheart, okay.'

'Sure Dad, no problem. I'd better dash, dinner to prepare and everything.'

'Okay Mary, speak soon, Love you, bye.'

There went his moment of normality.

He leaned into his desk and googled Hugo's Casino, a listing flashed up on his screen in seconds, he clicked on the link that would take him to their website and up it came on the screen. He had never been there, gambling did not interest him, it was a mugs game. The website had pictures of the roulette tables, glamourous staff and general information about the place. The text made it sound the place to be, as did the pictures of people in dinner jackets around the tables. All cleverly put together to lure naïve punters.

Then there was a picture of the owner and a bio about him. Hugo Martinez. Frank stared at the screen for a moment, not believing what he was seeing.

'Wait a minute – hold the phone,' he said aloud. 'Martinez! Martin – Marty,' he said, remembering Ryan's dying words. 'Could it be this was the man who David Ryan was referring to?'

Chapter Seven

The next morning, Mr Robinson called into Frank's office to examine the photographic evidence of his wife's apparent infidelity. Frank welcomed him and asked him to take a seat at his desk. The man was nervous, not wanting to face the reality of seeing the proof of his suspicion. Frank, though, had a knack of putting people at ease and relaxing them.

'Can I get you some coffee, Mr Robinson? I was just about to have one myself.'

'No thanks, Mr Doyle, let's just get this over with.' The man was slender with a gaunt face, and it seemed, of a slightly nervous disposition, not at all like the man Frank had seen with his wife the day before. Frank had learned from their first meeting that he was an accountant. Frank could not help feeling that his wife, judging by her appearance, was not a good match for him. She was rather racy, whereas he, tamely, but expensively dressed, looked like he had class.

Frank drew the file from the cabinet behind his desk and laid it down. He took his seat and began to take out the photographs. He paused for a moment.

'I realise this will be upsetting for you, just take your time.' He continued to pull the images from the file and placed them before his client. He got up from his swivel chair and poured himself some coffee, giving the man a moment alone to absorb the images of his wife and apparent lover.

Frank returned to his desk; the man was silent for a moment as he studied the evidence. He brushed away a tear as he stared at the photographs, unable it seemed, to take his eyes away. But then he spoke. Slowly looking up from them, he looked at Frank. 'I've seen this man before,' he said, mildly.

'Then you know him? I'm afraid to say that's not unusual in this type of case, Mr Robinson.'

'No, I don't know him. But I've seen him somewhere. If only I could remember where, Mr Doyle.'

'Maybe it'll come to you. But don't worry, I'm sure I'll be able to find out his identity soon.'

'I still can't believe it. How could she do this to me, I've given her everything she wanted,' he said. They were words that Frank had heard time and time again from a husband or wife in his situation. 'What shall I do? I still love her, God help me.'

'I wish I had a simple answer to that, Mr Robinson, but everyone handles these things in different ways,' said Frank, 'personally, I'd advise you confront her with these photographs and see what she has to say. After that, it's up to you what path you take. I will, of course, be here for you, should you need me.'

'Thanks, Mr Doyle,' said the man, raising from the chair, 'I'll be in touch.'

'Okay, sir, and I'm very sorry. And if you remember where you've seen this man, give me a call, okay. Oh, and I've prepared the bill for you.' Frank handed him an envelope.

'Thank you. And I will call you if I remember anything. Goodbye, Mr Doyle.'

It was not until the afternoon that Frank received a call on his cell phone while on another surveillance case. He was once again parked outside a motel. Pretty standard stuff. He recognised the number as his Mr Robinson.

'Frank Doyle speaking,'

'Mr Doyle, it's Eric Robinson,' he said, excitedly.

'What can I do for you, Mr Robinson?'

'I remembered where I've seen that man in the photograph.'

'Go on.'

'It was at the casino. I'm not a gambler you understand, but Sherrie seemed to like going there. She liked playing the roulette table. I couldn't stand it personally, not my kind of place at all, so much so that sometimes I'd let her go on her own. Come to think of it, I think she preferred it that way.'

'Hugo's Casino?' asked Frank.

'Of course, it's the only casino around here.'

'Well, was this man a customer of the casino, or an employee?'

'Oh, he worked there, no doubt about it. I'm going there to confront him.'

'Oh, I strongly advise against it, Mr Robinson. I'll go along there myself to find out who this guy is. Have you spoken to your wife about this yet?'

'I'm at the office, I haven't had a chance yet. But Mr Doyle, I want to see this man in person.'

'I know you do, but I've seen the guy, he looks pretty mean.'

'I don't care how mean he looks, I just want to see him in person.'

'I can see I'm not going to be able to talk you out of it. At least let me come along with you.'

The man could see the sense in Frank's argument. 'Yes, okay, if you think it's for the best.'

'I do. Now when were you thinking of going there?'

'Tonight.'

'Okay, come to my office at 9 to pick me up.'

'Very well, I'll see you then, Mr Doyle.'

'Just one thing, Mr Robinson, there'll be no confrontation. We handle this my way or not at all. At this stage, all we want is his name if possible.'

'Very well, if you say so.'

Frank was astounded at the coincidence. The very place he intended to pay a visit to, and now this. It would make his job a good deal easier, he thought. He could snoop a little, ask a few questions perhaps, with a perfect cover. That was, if he could control his client. He seemed uncharacteristically brave and excitable and that could be a problem, he thought.

There was nothing to report on his latest case, the woman emerged from the motel alone. Frank followed her back to her home address, then called it a day and returned once again to his office.

Frank no sooner set foot in his office when he got a call from John McKay. 'Hi John, what's up?' asked Frank.

'Well, I'm off duty and I wondered if you'd like to meet for a drink tonight?'

'That'd be swell, but I'm afraid I can't, not tonight.'

'Sure. Anyway, I wanted to apologise for balling you out the other day. You know how it is, sometimes the pressure of work gets to you.'

'Forget it, Buddy.'

'Well, that was all I called for. Maybe another time eh Frank?'

'Look forward to it. See you around, John.'

'See you, Frank.'

Frank thought that by the reserved tone of voice of his friend, he had something on his mind. Something other than the usual pressure of the job. Almost immediately, his phone rang again.

'Frank Doyle speaking.'

'Hello, Mr Doyle, it's Sandra Gray, we met the other night, you said I could call you anytime.'

'Of course, Miss Gray, what can I do for you. Have you thought of anything?'

'I'm afraid not. I was wondering if you'd had any luck.'

'Well, I may have a small lead, it's too early to say for sure and I don't want to get your hopes up.'

'Can you tell me what it is?'

'As I say, it's too early, but if it comes to anything, I'll be sure to let you know – that I promise. How are you coping, anyway?'

'Not so good, Mr Doyle. If only I knew why David was killed.'

'I know, it must be tough. As soon as I get something…'

'Alright. Thank you, Mr Doyle. Goodbye.'

Frank felt bad that he had not shared his lead with the young woman, yet he knew it was for the best if he were to proceed with his investigation successfully. It was going to be difficult enough keeping an outraged husband under control, without a grieving girlfriend as well.

He locked up his office and went upstairs to his apartment. It had been another long day and it was not over yet.

His Mr Robinson was an accountant alright. It was on the stroke of 9 when Frank heard his door intercom buzz. He answered it and said he would be right down.

Frank had dug out a dark grey suit that he hardly ever wore, a pale blue shirt and tie. He was surprised to see Mr Robinson casually dressed in beige pants and a similarly coloured windcheater. Was he going prepared for a fight? One thing was for sure, he would not blend in amid the dinner jackets and suits.

'Good evening, Mr Doyle,' he said, politely as ever.

'Good evening.'

'Well, this is it then,' said Robinson.

'Look, Mr Robinson, I think it'd be best if you let me do the talking – if there's any talking to be done, that is. I hope you're not thinking of creating a scene, because if you are, you can count me out. This needs to be handled with care.'

'I just want to speak to this man, Mr Doyle, that's all,' he said, concentrating on the road.

'As long as there's no violence – besides, he'd kill you.'

'We'll see about that.'

Frank suspected the worst. He knew how badly an outraged husband or wife could react to such bad news. 'Mr Robinson, tell me you're not carrying a gun.'

The man's silence spoke volumes. This was beginning to look like a bad idea.

Frank waited until they had arrived at the casino's parking lot. He quickly got out of the car and grabbed Robinson, feeling inside his jacket pockets, and sure enough, there it was, a 9mm pistol. Frank took the gun.

'That's pretty dumb! Frank said angrily, 'You were going to implicate me in murder and that makes me angry, Mr Robinson. Besides, you wouldn't have stood a chance of getting in there carrying a gun. You must know, having been here before that these places have metal detectors at the door for just that reason.'

Robinson looked shaken by Frank's roughness and harsh words. And in that moment, it was as if he came back to reality. 'I'm sorry, Mr Doyle, I don't know what came over me, I wasn't thinking straight.'

'No, you weren't, were you? Okay, well, we'll just put this in the car for now. Now, once we're in there – behave, okay.'

The man nodded and they went in.

'Remember, leave this to me,' Frank said, as they passed through security. He glanced at the photo of the man in question. He had also brought along the photo of David Ryan. This was the case that truly captured his imagination.

Chapter Eight

The casino was buzzing, the first room, a large area, had hundreds of slot machines, most were in use by hopeful punters continually feeding the hungry machines. The noise was deafening, the room brightly lit from artificial lighting on a high ceiling and there were no windows. As they wandered the crowded floor, Frank wondered why anyone could become so obsessed with such a pastime. To him, it seemed senseless, the house was almost always going to win. The place had a glitzy décor, a pseudo glamourous look which attracted vulnerable gamblers. He turned to Robinson who was by his side.

'You said that your wife liked the roulette tables?'

'Yes, that's right,' said Robinson.

'Where are they?' Frank asked.

'The tables are in the next room, through those doors over there,' he said, pointing to some large oak-panelled doors on the opposite side of the room.

'Well, let's go take a look,' said Frank, all the time scanning the room for their man.

A member of staff, dressed in a dinner suit, greeted them and opened the door for them to enter the part of the casino where the big money gamblers played. It was sumptuous in contrast to the slots room, with thick carpet and low, atmospheric lighting.

'Go and buy a few chips,' said Frank.

Robinson obeyed and a few minutes later, returned with a handful of chips. 'What now?'

'You play.'

'I've never played roulette in my life,' said Robinson.

'I thought you came here with your wife?'

'Yes, but it was her that played, not me, I only ever watched.'

'Just watch the other players for a moment. You're an accountant, you should be able to pick up some clues, just try it. Now you stay right here, I'm going to take a look around.'

'Very well, if you say so.'

'I won't be long, good luck on the table.'

Besides the roulette tables, there were many people seated at small tables scattered around the room, having drinks. Frank chose a table and sat down. He had no sooner done so when a waiter came to him and asked if he could get him anything. He ordered a beer. Frank had positioned himself so that he had a good all-round view of the room, including the roulette table where Robinson stood peering over the shoulders of some of the seated players.

There was an elevator door fairly close to where he sat. Frank guessed it might lead to the office of Martinez. He observed it closely.

An hour passed and Frank had made his beer at its inflated price, last. He had not seen their man, and Robinson was now seated at the roulette table, playing. It was as if he had forgotten the reason he was there, which suited Frank nicely. But suddenly, Frank heard the elevator spring into action and moments later, the door opened and a man stepped out. He instantly recognised him as the man he had seen with Robinson's wife at the motel.

The man stopped and looked around him as he exited the elevator. He looked a mean piece of work, that was for sure. The waiter came brushing past Frank's table, but Frank stopped him and ordered another beer.

'Before you go,' said Frank to the waiter, 'that man over there, I'm sure I know him, but I can't quite remember his name. I'd love to go over and speak to him, but you know how it is, it's embarrassing when you can't remember someone's name.'

'Certainly sir, that's Robert Downes, I believe. He works upstairs.'

'Of course! Thank you.' Frank stuffed ten dollars in the waiter's hand for the information.

'Thank you, sir, I'll bring your drink in a moment.'

There was never any intention of confronting the man. Frank had all he needed – a name. Now he could easily check him out for an address, which could be used in the event of any divorce proceedings. Job done! The waiter came back shortly with Frank's beer. Robert Downes had left by now.

'There you are, sir, there's your beer. Did you get to speak to Mr Downes?'

'No, I'll speak to him another time, he looked in a hurry. But there is one other thing you may be able to help me with before you go.'

'What's that, sir?'

Frank took out the photo of David Ryan and showed him. 'Have you seen this man here before?' he asked.

'Are you a cop or something?' asked the waiter with a half-smile.

'Something! Have you seen him?'

'Look, I'm just a waiter, I don't want to lose my job. Who is this guy, anyway?'

'You're not going to lose your job; this is between you and me. Take another look at the picture.'

The young man looked around him nervously, knowing very well that every square inch of the room was monitored by CCTV. He glanced quickly at the photo again.

'Yeah, I've seen him here several times. He played the tables big time. Is that it? Now, if you'll excuse me, I've got work to do.' And with that, he hurried off.

The information was enough for now, Frank thought. At least he knew that this was where Ryan did his gambling. He was on the right track, it seemed.

At that moment, Robinson found Frank sat at the table and rushed over excitably. 'I'm up a hundred-dollars,' he said. Another gambling addict in the making? Frank wondered.

'Well, that's great,' said Frank, dismissively.

'What about you, Mr Doyle, did you manage to find out anything?'

'Yep, we've got a name to the face. He is one Robert Downes. All I need to do is run a check on the name, and get his address, then it's up to you. You can now name him in the divorce proceedings – if that's the way you intend to go.'

'I've had time to think this evening and if he's the type of guy she wants, then he's welcome to her. Well done Mr Doyle, I appreciate it.'

'You're welcome. I'll just finish my beer while you're cashing in those chips of yours.'

'Yes, of course.'

They left the roulette room and once again found themselves in the area for slots. As they were leaving the building, Frank noticed that the man he now knew to be Robert Downes was heading straight for them as he came back into the casino. Downes brushed immediately past the two of them, yet the face did not register with Robinson. His and Frank's eyes met for the briefest of moments as they passed one another. Frank thought he must be at least 6'2" tall with a physique to match. He seemed to tower over Frank's 5'11"

The two men reached Robinson's car and they left.

The waiter called over to Robert Downes as he entered the roulette room and headed for the elevator.

'Mr Downes, Mr Downes, sir.'

'Yeah, what is it kid?' he said, straightening his bow tie.

'Uh.'

'Well, what is it kid? I'm a busy man.'

'Uh, well, I just thought you should know that there was a guy asking about you.'

'Oh really? Asking what exactly?'

'Well, nothing much. He just wanted to know your name, but I didn't tell him anything,' said the young man, lying.

'Where is this guy? Is he still here?'

'No, he just left with some other guy. You just missed him.'

'What did he look like?'

'Well, he was a bit overweight, medium height, I'd say. The guy he was with was kinda weedy though. I think he was a cop, 'cos he was asking about someone else too.'

'Who?'

'A punter I think, don't know his name. But I recognised the guy, he showed me a picture.'

'I think I may have passed these guys on my way in,' Downes said, thinking aloud. 'Okay, kid, thanks.' He took a twenty from his money clip and gave it to the waiter as he entered the elevator. 'And if you see this guy again, call me upstairs, okay?'

'Yes, sir. Thank you, sir.'

The elevator door opened into Martinez's office. Martinez, as was his habit during the evening was found to be lounging on a large leather couch, drinking champagne along with two of his favourite girls.

'Someone's been asking questions about me downstairs. Could be a cop. I don't like it.'

'Hey, relax. Come and have some champagne.'

'I don't feel like champagne. I'm worried.'

'Look, Bobby, you know as well as I do, it can't possibly be a cop, and even if it was, I pay them extremely well, so relax. But I'll tell you what we'll do. If it makes you feel any better, we'll examine the CCTV tape tomorrow, to see if we can ID this guy. Now, come on, have some champagne.'

'By all accounts, he was also asking about one of the punters – I don't know who, but it may have been Ryan.'

'Yes, that put's a slightly different light on the matter. I don't like it when people ask questions about my customers,' Martinez said, rising from the sofa. 'Never fear though, Bobby, we'll get to the bottom of this, I guarantee it.'

Chapter Nine

A couple of uneventful days went by. It was early evening when Frank decided to pay another visit to O'Malley's bar. He did not have high hopes of getting any further information, but it had been another long day and he felt in the mood to unwind with a beer anyway. He arrived to find his friend, Pete on duty, he had not had the opportunity to speak to him about Ryan yet.

The bar was reasonably busy, but not so busy that he could not find a seat at the bar.

'Hey Frank, good to see you.'

'You too.'

'The usual, Frank?'

'Yeah, creature of habit, that's me.'

'Bad business about David Ryan, wasn't it? I just wish I could have helped him. I was working during the day you know,' said Pete, pouring out Frank's beer into a glass.

'Yeah, Danny told me. Did he say anything about what was bothering him? Anything at all?'

'No, Frank, he didn't want to talk. He just got quietly drunk. Oh, I tried to talk to him alright, it was pretty obvious he had something big on his mind, but he didn't want to know.'

'It was you that found him wasn't it, Frank?'

'Yeah, I'm afraid so.'

'What do you make of it? I read in the paper that the police were treating it as a chance killing. But with the way he was behaving that day, I don't believe that, not for a second. He looked to me like a man in trouble.'

'No, me neither, that's why I'm looking into it myself.'

'Well, I'm glad someone is, and there's no one better than you, Frank. Have you got anything to go on?'

'Yeah, maybe something. Did you know he was a serious gambler?'

'Who, David? Never!'

'Well, I'm afraid he was, he had a serious problem, and I believe it has something to do with his murder.'

'Jesus, I had no idea. Do you know if his girlfriend knows?'

'Sandra Gray? She does now.'

'Poor kid, they used to come in together sometimes. They always seemed really happy. Just goes to show, doesn't it, you never really know what goes on behind closed doors.'

'Ain't that the truth.'

'You never can tell about people, Frank.'

'I understand he was a customs officer at the harbour?'

'Yeah, that's right, he had a pretty senior position, I think. Why do you ask?'

'Oh, no reason. Forget it.' Frank swallowed the last of his beer.

'Same again, Frank?'

'No thanks, Pete, think I'll head off. I'll see you.'

'Take care, Frank.'

Before going to his car, Frank stood outside O'Malley's and lit a cigar. He took a great lungful of smoke, then blew it out in a cloud that filled the cool night air. He glanced at the alleyway where he had found Ryan. It was a dead-end alley where O'Malley's kept their dumpsters. What a place to die, thought Frank.

He got in his car, wound down the window, and drove home without any further material to work on. Pete was not only a friend, but a reliable source of information. Frank knew if he'd had anything useful to add, he would have told him. Frank decided that his next visit would be to the customs office where Ryan worked. He would go there tomorrow.

Frank arrived outside his apartment at around 10.30pm, still puffing on the remainder of his cigar. He entered his apartment, feeling for the light switch, located it and turned on the lights. He was fairly certain he had left a light burning when he went out earlier. He flung his jacket down on the sofa and made his way to the kitchen to get some coffee, stopping briefly to turn on his record deck and putting on some smooth jazz by Charlie Parker. He hummed to the tune of "Everything Happens to Me" as he put the kettle on the gas hob and came back into the living room.

'Good evening, Mr Doyle, we've been waiting for you,' said a man, lounging on Frank's sofa, his crocodile skin boots resting on one end. Frank instantly recognised him from the casino's website as Hugo Martinez. Another man stood silently by the apartment's door; his arms folded. Frank also recognised him as Robert Downes.

'What the hell's going on?' said Frank. 'How did you get in here?'

'Not difficult, my friend. Not difficult at all.'

'Well, what do you want?'

'I should have thought that was obvious. Relax. Take a seat,' said Martinez. 'You do know who I am I suppose? And I'm certain you know who my friend is.'

'I don't know what you're talking about,' said Frank, acting dumb.

'Come now, don't insult my intelligence. Please take a seat.'

'I'll stand, if it's all the same to you.'

'Please yourself.'

'What do you want?' asked Frank, angrily.

'It's really very simple, Mr Doyle. You see, I don't like it when people start snooping on my staff – especially when that person is a private investigator. Why have you been asking questions about my friend here, may I ask?'

'I still don't know what you're talking about.'

'That's a shame, a great shame.' He gestured to Downes, 'Bobby!'

The man slowly approached Frank. In his hand was a long piece of twine. Frank's heart stopped for a moment.

He was almost relieved when the man pushed him into a seat and tied his hands behind his back with the twine.

'There, that's much better,' said Martinez, 'I hope now, I have your attention.'

'I don't know how many times I have to say it. I don't know what you're talking about,' said Frank, boldly.

Martinez sighed and nodded to his friend. 'I think our friend here needs a little more convincing,' he said to Downes.

The man punched Frank hard in the stomach twice. Frank groaned in pain.

'Is anything coming back to you?' said Martinez. Frank said nothing and Martinez nodded to his friend again.

This time, the man concentrated on Frank's face. He punched him hard several times until blood streamed from his lip and a cut opened above his right eye. Frank abhorred violence, but he was tough, he barely flinched.

'Well?' asked Martinez. 'Anything to say now?'

'It's a divorce case. Your ape man here happens to be having an affair with my client. I needed to identify him. That's all there is to it,' said Frank. 'Does the name Robinson mean anything to you, Bobby?' asked Frank.

'Well, does it Bobby?' asked Martinez.

'Just some blonde bimbo, that's all boss.'

'Very well,' said Martinez, 'but you're forgetting one thing aren't you Mr Doyle. Bobby here isn't the only person you've been asking about in my casino, is he?' Frank said nothing.

Martinez stood up. 'Untie him,' he instructed. 'Mr Doyle, you're clearly a brave man, but take this as a warning, a gentle warning. I don't want to see you in my casino ever again. Do I make myself clear?'

'Crystal.'

'Good, then we have an understanding, yes?'

Frank nodded. The pain in his jaw was beginning to set in.

'I'm glad you agree. And with that in mind, I'll leave you now. Please don't forget this little chat will you Mr Doyle, you'll find I'm not a man to play games with.'

'I'll try to remember that,' said Frank, defiantly.

'Good-evening and goodbye then Mr Doyle.'

The two men left, Martinez with a confident swagger, Bobby scowling at Frank as he closed the door behind them.

Frank bathed his blooded lip and applied a sticking plaster to the cut above his eye. He did not think stitches were necessary, but he had an almighty headache. However, the events of the evening had proved beyond a shadow of a doubt that Martinez was rattled. He had something to hide, and Frank was certain it was murder.

He had a long soak in the bath, his gun now close to hand since his unwelcome visitors. He could not help feeling there was yet more to discover about Hugo Martinez, and now it had become personal.

Chapter Ten

The next morning, Frank's headache had subsided, but the wound over his eye was stinging like hell and he had developed bruising to his face and ribs. He made some coffee and scrambled eggs for his breakfast before continuing his enquiries. Even before Martinez and his heavy had broken into his apartment and roughed him up, he had decided to pay a visit to the U.S. Customs office at the harbour. He was not sure if they would be willing to speak about a deceased employee or even if they would be able to tell him anything useful, but it was worth a try, he thought.

After a second cup of coffee, he got dressed, it was the second time in the space of a few days he had worn his smartest suit. He thought it best to make an appointment, rather than turn up unannounced. That was, if they agreed to speak to him. He looked up the telephone number in the directory and dialled the number.

'CBP – Port Authority,' answered a young woman on the switchboard.

'Good morning, my name is Frank Doyle. I wondered if I could make an appointment to speak to someone regarding David Ryan?'

'Oh, you mean the young man who was killed? I'm not sure, if you would hold for a moment, I'll find out.'

Frank was forced to listen to some awful generic music while he was put on hold. Luckily it was not too many minutes before someone answered.

'Hello, Mr Doyle, is it?'

'That's correct, sir.'

'I understand you want to speak to someone about David Ryan. I was his line manager, what was it you wanted to know? Are you a police officer?' the man asked quizzically.

'No sir, I'm a private investigator. Well, sir, I would like to speak to you and anyone that knew David, in person, if possible.'

'But I thought that the police had virtually closed the case.'

'That may be so, but I believe there was more to it. It may even have involved his work. His position may have been compromised, so you see, it might be to your advantage as well.'

'Very well, could you come along at 11.00am, I'll have a visitors badge waiting for you at reception. Ask for Officer Brown.'

'Thanks, I appreciate it. See you at 11.00'

Frank arrived at the office's reception desk just before 11am. 'Morning, I have an appointment with Officer Brown at eleven, my name's Frank Doyle.'

'Oh yes, Mr Doyle, we spoke earlier. Here's your visitor's badge. I'll call Mr Brown now for you. Terrible about Mr Ryan.' She pushed a button on her switchboard and spoke through the microphone on her headset. 'Mr Doyle here to see you, sir. Okay, yes, I'll do that.' She flicked off the button and spoke to Frank. 'Mr Brown will be down to see you shortly, if you'd care to take a seat, I'm sure he won't be long.'

'Thanks. Did you know David Ryan?' he asked the receptionist.

'No, not well. Just enough to say "Hi" really.'

'I see,' said Frank.

'But you should find plenty of his fellow officers on duty who did know him,' she said, helpfully.

'Thanks, that's good to know.'

At that moment, the officer, in his uniform and crisp white shirt complete with epaulettes, walked down the stairs and greeted Frank. The large reception area was empty of people. 'Nice to meet you, Mr Doyle.' He sat down facing him. 'Jesus, what happened to you?' he said.

'Oh, nothing much, just a slight accident,' Frank replied.

'I see, now, what can I do for you? What do you want to know exactly? You said something on the phone about this possibly being to my advantage, what did you mean?'

'Well, there's no reason why you should know this, but it seems David Ryan was being blackmailed,' said Frank.

The man sat up straighter. 'Blackmailed, no, surely not. The police never mentioned it. Maybe we should continue this conversation in my office.'

'Yeah, maybe you're right,' said Frank.

Frank followed the officer to the first floor and entered his office that overlooked the harbour.

'Now, as I was saying, Mr Doyle, the police didn't mention anything about David being blackmailed.

'Hmm, I'm not sure what form the blackmail was taking myself at the moment, but for someone in his position, well, you understand it could possibly have involved his work here.'

'Yes, yes, I can see that.'

'Did you know him well?' asked Frank.

'Yes, pretty well, I think. It was a real shock to hear about his death, and murder at that.'

'You didn't see anything unusual in his behaviour over the past few months?'

'I Can't say I did, no. Well, there was one thing. It may mean nothing, but he did request a lot of shift changes, and as you say, over the last few months. That was unusual for him.'

'Uh huh, I see. Tell me, does the name Martinez mean anything to you, Hugo Martinez?'

'Only that he owns the casino, just out of town, and of course, that he has a yacht moored here in the harbour. Why do you ask?'

'Just an idea at the moment. I'll keep you informed if it comes to anything. Does David have any colleagues that might also be regarded as a friend here today?'

'Yes, I think so, Alec Mundy. He'll be in the harbour at the moment.'

'Do you mind if I speak to him?'

'No, go ahead, if it helps.'

'Thank you, Officer Brown, I won't keep you any longer.'

'I just hope I was of some help.'

'I can hardly believe how helpful you've been. Thanks again. Oh, one other thing, do you happen to know the name of Martinez yacht?'

'Yes, I do, it's "Lady of The Sea."'

Frank jotted the name down in is notebook and made his way to the harbour. It was not long before he saw a man, he guessed was in his thirties in uniform speaking to someone in the harbour. It was a bright day, but the breeze from the sea was cool. He made his way over to him just as the conversation was ending.

'Alec Mundy?' Frank shouted over to him.

'Yes, that's right, and you are?'

Frank reached the man and introduced himself. 'Frank Doyle, I've just been speaking to your boss, he told me it would be okay to have a word with you.'

'A word. What about?' asked the slim, dark haired young man.

'Relax,' said Frank, 'I just want to ask you about David Ryan, Officer Brown said you were friends.'

'Are you from the police?'

'No, I'm working in a private capacity. I'm a private investigator.'

'I thought for a moment the police were at last going to ask me some questions about David. They haven't yet you know.'

'No, I'm sure they haven't.'

'They don't seem interested,' said Alec.

'I know, look, I just wanted to know if you'd noticed any change in his behaviour recently?'

'Sure, he wasn't the David I knew. He had something on his mind alright.'

'But he never told you what it was, right?'

'That's right. Oh, I asked him plenty of times, but he'd never talk about it.'

'And he changed shifts a lot just lately I understand.'

'Yeah, he swapped with me several times in the last few months. He wanted the night shift sometimes, which I found odd, but it suited me just fine, so we swapped.'

'And those dates will be on record?'

'Oh yeah, sure.'

'Thanks Alec, here's my card if you think of anything, no matter how small. If you've got a moment, I'd like to see the yacht belonging to Hugo Martinez. Could you take me there do you think?'

'Sure, it's just along here a short way, why the interest in Martinez's yacht?'

'It's nothing more than a hunch at the moment, I can't say any more than that.'

They strolled along the waterfront until a few minutes later, they reached the mooring. Lady of The Sea, was a fifty-foot luxury yacht, Alec told Frank, but it was not present, and Frank's instincts told him that it played some part in the murder of David Ryan. The feeling was strong. All he had to do now, was find the connection. Easier said than done. Especially now his life was in danger as well.

'There aren't any floodlights in this area,' Frank said, sharing his observation with Alec.

The young man looked around him. 'You know, I hadn't thought anything of it before, but you're right, there aren't.'

'Do you happen to know how often this yacht goes out to sea?' asked Frank.

'Pretty often, I think. And for a couple of weeks at a time too.'

'I take it, all of this would be on your records?'

'Yes, of course. I could dig them out and let you know, if you like.'

'That'd be great. And would you be able to cross-reference that with David's shift patterns?'

'No problem.'

'I'll wait to hear from you then, said Frank.'

'Yeah, I'll get onto it today.'

Frank said no more, but shook Alec's hand and thanked him.

Chapter Eleven

Back at his office, Frank checked his answering machine while making coffee. There were a few calls from current and prospective clients. The last message was from Sandra Gray asking if they could meet. The message was timed at 1.15pm, he guessed it would have been during her lunch break. It was now 2pm. He decided to call her back after office hours.

In the meantime, he called a lock and security company. He had given them a great deal of work for nervous clients that wanted extra security for one reason or another. He asked for them to visit his apartment to fit some extra locks. It had been all too easy for Martinez and his man, Downes, to pick his lock the night before, and he did not want a repeat performance. The company was always busy, but said they would come the next day.

But now it was time to do some work, the kind of work that paid the bills. It was yet another matrimonial case. A suspicious wife this time. The husband involved had, by all accounts taken to working late a little too often for her liking, and it was Frank's job to find out if he was telling the truth or not. Frank had details, such as the address of the man's office, his make of car and registration, and of course, a clear photograph of him.

The man worked in a large office block in the financial district. Frank drove there and located the car in the office's parking lot. He parked nearby and waited, camera at the ready. At 6pm, the wait was over as the man approached his car, got in and drove off in a hurry. Frank followed at a safe distance until they arrived outside an apartment block in Western Avenue, not far from Harvard's campus. The man left his car and Frank discreetly followed him into the apartment block. He was a good-looking guy in his late forties or early fifties. Frank held back in second-floor passage as the man rang the doorbell. A much younger woman came out to greet him, flinging her arms around him. Frank waited for them to go inside and then made a note of the apartment number.

Frank returned to his vehicle and waited. It could, he thought, be a long wait. He searched his wallet for Sandra Gray's business card and dialled her cell phone number. She answered, her voice naturally betraying a great sadness.

'Sandra Gray.'

'Hi Sandra, it's Frank Doyle, you called me earlier today. Is everything okay?'

'Yes, Frank, I'm okay. I was wondering if we could meet for a drink, that's all.'

'Yeah, of course, when did you have in mind?'

'I was thinking this evening perhaps, but if you're busy…'

'Not at all. Where?'

'Somewhere convenient for both of us, I was thinking, O'Malley's bar.'

'Sure, shall we say 8 O'clock?'

'That'd be great, thanks Frank.'

'My pleasure, I'll see you there at eight then.'

Frank found it a strange choice for a place to meet. the place outside of which, her boyfriend had been murdered, but who was he to question it? He waited outside the apartment block for another hour. There was still no sign of the man leaving, so he gave up, making a note of the time his surveillance ended.

He made his way across town to O'Malley's and arrived just after 8.00. He found Sandra at the spot where David had lost his life, she had laid flowers. He looked on from fifteen-yards away, not wishing to disturb her personal moment. She sensed a presence and looked round at Frank.

'Frank,' she said, shivering a little from the cool evening air.

'Sandra. I'm sorry I'm late. Are you okay?'

'Yes,' she sniffed.

'Shall we go in?' said Frank, gently taking her arm.

Once inside, they found a quiet table and sat down. The bar was busy, as it usually was during the evenings. The atmosphere was great for winding down after a hard day, with its low lighting and on this particular evening, jazz was being played by a local band at the far end of the bar.

'How have you been?' asked Frank.

'Oh, I still can't quite bring myself to believe it, you know how it is?'

'Yeah, I know exactly what you mean. It'll take time.'

'It's not just David dying the way he did. It's the fact we were living a lie for so long and not knowing who did this that's really getting to me.'

'I understand. Hopefully, I'll be able to help.'

'My God, Frank, I'm sorry, I'm so full of self-pity, what on earth happened to you? Have you been in a fight?' she said, his cuts and bruises only now becoming apparent to her.

'A one-sided one I'm afraid.'

'What do you mean?'

'I'm on to something, Sandra…'

'What can I get you folks?' Neither Frank, nor Sandra recognised the waiter.

'I'll have a glass of your house red,' said Sandra.

'And I'll have a Bud – with a glass.'

'You were saying?' said Sandra, after the waiter had left.

'Have you heard of Hugo Martinez, the casino owner?'

'Yes, of course. He has an account at my bank, a huge account, I believe.'

'Really? That may prove useful.'

'What's going on Frank? What has this to do with David?'

'You said, David told you he was being blackmailed. Well, it's really quite simple, I think Martinez was the one blackmailing him.'

'Why would he do that?'

'Well, I'm pretty sure it was Martinez who David got into debt with. The rest, is a little cloudier, but I think it had something to do with David's job. Martinez needed him for something.'

'Oh, come on Frank, this all sounds a little far-fetched to me. Where's your proof? Why would he need David?''

'This is all the proof I need for now,' he said, pointing to his wounds.

'Are you saying Martinez did this to you?'

'He and one of his boys broke into my apartment after I'd been sniffing around at the casino asking questions. No, Martinez didn't get his hands dirty, but he gave the order.'

'Oh my God, Frank, I'm so sorry,' said Sandra.

Say, would you like to eat? I haven't eaten since breakfast.'

'Well, maybe just a bite,' she said, picking up the menu. Frank had already decided he was having one of O'Malley's famous burgers.

Sandra slapped the menu on the table. 'You really believe that David was somehow involved with Martinez, don't you Frank?'

'Yes, I do,' he said, bluntly.

'Good enough. I trust you. But I can't begin to imagine how he would be involved. If there's anything I can do to help…'

'Here you go, one red wine and one Bud. Would you like to order some food?'

'Yes,' said Frank, eagerly. He gestured to Sandra.

'I'll just have the cheese salad.'

'And I'll have your special burger with a side order of fries.'

'Good choice, I'll be back soon.'

'There may be something you could do,' said Frank.

'Yes, what?' she said, keenly, eager to help, and glad of a possible distraction.

'But only if you could do it without getting into trouble.'

'So, it would involve my job, is that what you're saying?'

'Yeah, I'm afraid it would.'

'Tell me what you want me to do.'

'Would you have access to accounts?'

'Yes, I take it we're talking about Martinez's account?'

'Uh huh, that's right. Could you do that undetected?'

'Not exactly. You see, when I log on to my terminal each day, it automatically logs everything I've done – every account I've looked at and when. A footprint.'

'In that case, forget it, it's too risky.'

'What did you want to know anyway?'

'Any unusually large transactions with dates. But as I said, forget it. You're not doing it, end of story.'

'Just tell me one thing, Frank. Do you believe Martinez was behind David's death?'

'Yes, I do.'

'Then I'll do it!' Sandra said confidently.

'Out of the question,' insisted Frank.

'Is that your final word on the subject?'

'Yes, it is.'

'In that case…'

'Good, subject closed,' said Frank.

Chapter Twelve

The next morning, Frank got an early call from the security company asking whether it would be convenient for them to come along to fit the extra locks to his apartment door. He was pleased to arrange an appointment, and a man and his assistant duly arrived at 9.30am to do the work. Frank gave them coffee, explained what he wanted, and left them to their work. He went downstairs to his office to catch up on routine paperwork. It was the part of his job he disliked the most, but it had to be done. It reinforced his notion of employing an administrative assistant.

He set about compiling his report and photographic evidence based on his surveillance from the evening before. He made checks on the residency of apartment No 16, discovering that it was in the name of a young female and that the block was almost entirely occupied by students from Harvard who chose to live off campus. The meeting between her and his client's husband could have been quite innocent, although Frank doubted it.

His mind turned yet again though to the Ryan case. He was concerned about Sandra Gray delving into the

Martinez account. Could he trust her not to? The last thing he wanted was for her to be found out and lose her livelihood – he felt guilty for suggesting it. Nevertheless, if his instinct about Martinez was correct, then as much information as possible would help in building a strong case against him. The more background he had on Martinez, the less the police would be able to ignore it, he thought. Nevertheless, he hoped she took his advice and kept her nose clean.

At 11.00 a knock on the office door interrupted his thoughts. The locksmith's assistant entered.

'All done upstairs. Do you want to take a look?'

'Yeah, sure,' said Frank. They both went up to Frank's apartment.

'Hey Frank, what do you think? This should keep a two-ton gorilla out.'

'It may need to. Sounds like just what I need,' said Frank.

The locksmith had fitted two strong internal bolts and a keypad entry on the outside of the door.

'I've written the code down for you – happy?'

'Yeah, looks great, said Frank.

'Great! The office will send the bill, along with a discount for all the work you pass our way, okay, Frank.'

'Appreciate it.'

The two men left, once more leaving Frank with his thoughts on the Ryan case. He was convinced that Martinez had played a part in David Ryan's murder, yet without proof, the case was going nowhere. In a rare moment of despair, Frank felt helpless, not having police powers, he was not sure which direction to take. He picked up his phone and called John McKay on his cell phone.

'Mc Kay,' his friend answered.

'Hi John, it's Frank. I was wondering if you still wanted to meet for that drink?'

'Uh, yeah, sure Frank. That'd be great, I'm off duty today. Where'd you wanna meet?'

'I'll leave it up to you.'

'Well, how about, Joe's Bar, Dalton Street. You know it?'

'Yeah sure, 1 o'clock okay with you?'

'Yeah, sounds good. I'll see you there, Frank.'

Frank peered through the blinds of his office window. The day had suddenly become overcast and it was beginning to rain. Around one and a half hours later, as he pulled up and parked his vehicle some forty-yards away from the bar, there was a sudden cloudburst and he made a dash for the door. He had taken the precaution of putting on a raincoat before he left, yet in just a few moments he was drenched.

Once inside, he took off the raincoat and shook it before hanging it up. Frank looked around the dimly lit bar and saw John McKay already sitting in a booth. He was drinking what looked like a glass of whisky.

'Raining, Frank?'

'How'd you guess,' Frank laughed, as he took a seat in the booth opposite McKay.

'So, How's things, Frank?'

'Oh, yeah, fine.'

'So, what's the story on this?' McKay said, gesturing to Frank's facial wounds.

'Would you believe me if I said I walked into a door.'

'No Frank, I wouldn't. What have you been up to?'

The two men stared at one another for what seemed like a long time. It was as though they were trying to read one another's minds.

'So, how did you really get these cuts and bruises? What have you gotten into now?'

'I think it's probably best I keep that to myself, John, don't you?'

'Look, we've been friends a long time, Frank. I know you of old. Has this got anything to do with the Ryan case?'

'It may have,' said Frank, as he ordered a large beer from the waiter.

'Listen Frank, forget it, okay. I don't get why you're so interested anyway.'

'I used to be a cop remember, and good cops don't like to see people getting away with murder – do they John?'

'Don't come the high and mighty, Frank. It's out of my hands and I'm a married man, I can't go rocking the boat, I have my pension to think about.' McKay took a large swallow of his whisky.

'So, you're hiding something, is that it?'

'Not me, Frank.'

'Then who?'

McKay did not answer, he began to appear flustered and fidgeted. 'I thought this drink was supposed to be a social one. So enough with the questions, okay.'

'Who, John? All I want is a name. You have my word; I won't comprise you.'

'Someone at the top. That's all I'm saying, I've already said too much. It's not just my pension, Frank.'

'What do you mean?'

'It doesn't matter, don't concern yourself. Just stop digging Frank, for everyone's sake. Look, I'd better go now.'

'Stay and have another drink,' said Frank.

'I've gotta go,' John said, easing himself out of the booth. He flung a few dollars onto the table, looked steadily into Frank's eyes, then left.

Frank sat quietly, taking the occasional slow sip of beer, contemplating his friend's words, and allowing them to sink in. It seemed his suspicions were correct. Someone at the top may be taking cash from Martinez for protection. But again, he needed some firm proof, and that would not be so easy to obtain. John Mc Kay seemed terrified, was his life under threat as well?

Frank finished his beer, paid the check and left. The rain had lessened, was lighter, though the sky was still dark and gloomy. It somehow reflected his current mood. He was deeply concerned now for his friend's safety. He got into his car and took a slow drive back to his office. Thinking aloud as he drove, he said, 'Maybe for everyone's sake, I *should* drop it.'

He was feeling low when he returned. He decided to go straight to his apartment, he'd had enough for the day. He used the new entry system for the first time by tapping in the code he had been given, entered and made his way to the kitchen. Frank got himself a beer and made a sandwich. The disc he had been playing the night of his attack was still on the deck and he flicked it on, he needed to relax for a while.

Easing off his shoes, he put his feet up on the sofa, ate his sandwich, drank his beer and then drifted off to sleep. It seemed the best thing he could do after his meeting with John McKay. He hoped he had not lost a friend.

It was 6pm when he finally woke with a start as his cell phone rang next to him. It was Alec Mundy.

'Hello,' Frank answered, drowsily.

'Mr Doyle?'

'Yes, Frank Doyle speaking.'

'Mr Doyle, it's Alec Mundy from U.S. Customs. We spoke yesterday.'

'Yes, of course, hello Mr Mundy.'

'I'm calling to say that I did as you asked. I checked the dates and times, arrivals and departures of Martinez yacht, they have all been over the last four months. And guess what? those dates were always when David had switched shifts.'

'That's what I thought you'd say. You've been very helpful, Mr Mundy. Tell me, would it be possible to have a printout of these dates and times?'

'Yeah, sure. I'll bring it over to your office if you like.'

'That'd be great. Whenever it's convenient for you.'

'I could drop them to you after I finish my shift tomorrow morning, if that's okay.'

'Thanks a lot, Mr Mundy. Until tomorrow then.'

It was the best news Frank had had all day, good enough to break him out of his low mood. It did not alter his concern for Sandra, or for his continuing friendship with John McKay, but he looked forward to seeing the results of Alec Mundy's probing on paper. It should, he thought, prove extremely interesting, and might provide some of the proof that he badly needed to build a case against Martinez.

Yet apart from this good news, he felt that today, he had achieved nothing much, apart from alienating a good friend perhaps. There was nothing further he could do. He took out a ready-meal from the freezer and placed it in his microwave for five minutes. While it was cooking, he called his daughter to let her know he wouldn't be able to make lunch on Sunday. He did not wish to alarm her or his grandchildren with the injuries to his face. She was disappointed but understood when he told her he had to work on a case.

Chapter Thirteen

It was around 10am when Alec Mundy visited Frank at his office after finishing his night shift. Frank greeted him with some anticipation as he entered.

'Can I get you some coffee, Mr Mundy?' asked Frank.

'No thanks, call me Alec, by the way.'

'Likewise – call me Frank. Well, take a seat, Alec.'

'Thanks.' Alec opened his briefcase and took out the papers that could help nail Martinez. He spread them out on Frank's desk. 'Well, there it is, Frank. I think you'll see what I mean about the dates coinciding with David's change of shifts.'

Frank shuffled through the various papers, studying them carefully. 'Yeah, and it's interesting that they were always night shifts. Would I be right in saying that the Martinez yacht was out at sea for a month at a time?'

'Yeah, it sure appears that way.'

'And how far would you estimate a yacht like that could travel out of Boston and back in a month?'

'Oh, a yacht that size could cover some distance. Florida, even South America, Venezuela. Yeah, it could do that easily.'

'And the yacht is out at sea now?'

'Yeah, if the pattern we have is anything to go by, it should be due back in a matter of days.'

'Martinez has some kind of racket going on – I just wish I knew what it was,' said Frank.

'Drugs maybe?' asked Alec.

'That would be my guess, but I need to be certain.'

'Maybe you should inform the police,' said Alec.

'Yeah, but there's a problem – they don't seem interested in anything that concerns David's murder. I think the investigating team are in Martinez's pocket.'

'You're kidding me.'

'I wish I was.'

'What do you plan to do?'

'I'm not sure yet, but I may have another line of enquiry going on at the moment. Hopefully I should hear something soon.'

'Is there anything else I can do to help?'

'Maybe there is.'

'Just say the word, David was a friend, I want to help.'

'Well, maybe you could let me know when and if Martinez has any more trips scheduled. Though something tells me he won't have any just yet, not without David to assist his yacht's safe passage into the harbour.'

'Yeah, I get you. But if I do see anything, I'll be sure to let you know.'

'Thanks a lot, Alec. Is it okay if I keep these papers?'

'Yeah, sure,' said Alec, yawning.

'Okay, thanks. But right now, it looks like you could use some sleep.'

'You're not wrong, it was a long night. I'll be in touch, Frank.'

Frank held the door for Alec. 'Take care now,' said Frank, as Alec left.

Frank examined the papers again. He was convinced that Martinez was drug running into Boston. He placed them in a file and put it at the back of his cabinet, which he then locked. There was little else he could do, but wait to see if Sandra Gray came up with any useful information. Despite his warning to her, Frank somehow knew she would go ahead with her own investigation. Until that time, he would have to be content with routine work, he thought. He drank a cup of coffee before putting on a light jacket, it was a brighter and drier day than yesterday and he had the whereabouts of a couple of suspect husbands to check on.

Later that day, business was coming to a close at the First Boston Bank. Sandra sat at her desk in the upper floor office in a dream like state. She was snapped out of it as her female boss from the adjoining office put her head around the door to say goodbye for the day. She was leaving a little earlier than usual.

'Are you okay, Sandra? You looked miles away.'

'Yes, I'm fine, Karen. Just a little tired.'

Her boss entered the office. 'You know, I'd completely understand if you wanted to take some time off after all you've been through.'

'Thanks, Karen, I'd much rather be at work though, really I would. The last thing I need is to mope around in our – my apartment.'

'Well, just say the word, if you change your mind.'

'I will, I promise,' said Sandra with a forced smile.

'Why don't you call it a day? I certainly am, I'm going to the opera this evening.'

'Yes, I'll just tidy up a couple of things first. Thank you, Karen, enjoy the opera.'

'I will. Well, goodnight then.'

Sandra's boss's office was now locked, it would be impossible to access Martinez account from her terminal, it seemed she had no choice but to do it from her own terminal. It was not ideal. Martinez account was personally handled by Karen, should she find out it had been accessed by someone else, there would be questions and she was not sure how she would be able to answer.

Sandra hesitated over her terminal for a few moments. 'Well, here goes,' she said to herself. She logged on and attempted to access the Martinez account. She was rejected in seconds as the machine requested a password. She sat back in her chair to think. She typed in an answer, the name of Karen's dog, which immediately showed as incorrect. She took several other guesses, all were rejected.

She froze as she heard the door of Karen's office being opened. It was too early for the office cleaners.

With a sigh of relief, she heard it being locked once again, but then her door opened. Karen poked her head in again.

'Would you believe, I got to the ground floor and realised I'd left my purse behind.'

'Oh,'

'Anyway, you still here? I thought I told you to go home.'

'Just going,' said Sandra.

'Okay goodnight then.'

'Goodnight.'

Sandra breathed once again and resumed trying to find the correct password. Karens husband's name, her daughter's, none worked. Then she tried simply typing, Martinez – nothing. Her final and least likely, she thought, was Hugo. It let her in. 'That's a strange password to choose,' she said.

The man clearly had great wealth. She quickly scanned the amounts being paid in and out, but there was too much to take in and she was becoming very nervous. She took a memory stick from her desk, inserted it into the PC and proceeded to copy the details. Placing the stick in her purse, she hurriedly logged off and left her office. Sandra felt an illogical anxiety as she made her way in the elevator to the ground floor among some of her colleagues. She sighed with relief once out of the building.

Later that evening, Sandra, having processed the information in the comfort of her apartment, gave Frank a call on his cell phone. It was 10pm, it had taken her most of the evening to comprehend the wealth of Martinez.

'Frank, it's Sandra, sorry to disturb your evening, but I've got that information we talked about.'

'You have? I hope you didn't put yourself at risk. And don't worry about calling me, as I said before, you can call me at any time – day or night.'

'I'm not sure to be honest, Frank. But if it helps to catch David's killer…'

'Do you want me to come over?'

'I'll come to you, if that's okay? I could do with a drive to clear my head.'

'Sure, if that's what you want.'

'Okay, I'll see you in about thirty minutes. We're talking vast amounts of money, Frank.'

'That's what I thought. I'll be waiting for you in my office.'

Frank tidied up his desk of paperwork, made fresh coffee and waited, unaware his office and apartment were being watched.

Chapter Fourteen

'I'm sorry it's so late, but I thought you might want to see this as soon as possible,' said Sandra, as she entered Frank's office.

'Not a problem,' said Frank.

'I have the information on this memory stick,' she said, taking a seat at Frank's desk. Frank took the stick and inserted it into a USB point on his PC, clicked on the symbol and the file opened.

'I can see straight off what you were saying about vast amounts. I've never seen so many zeroes.'

'One thing's for sure, that amount of money couldn't all have come through his casino. He must have another source of income,' said Sandra.

'I agree.'

'You've probably already noticed the regularity of some of the larger payments over the past few months.'

'Yeah, I see what you mean. And all of them paid into his account with cash,' said Frank, turning the monitor so that Sandra could share the screen.

'Exactly,' agreed Sandra.

'I received some other interesting information this morning. I'll get it from the filing cabinet. I think we'll find that the dates of these payments coincide with the movements of Martinez yacht.'

'His yacht? What's the connection?'

Frank retrieved the paperwork given to him by Alec Mundy and took his seat again. 'I'll explain as clearly as I can in a moment. Take a look at these.' He handed her the papers that showed David's change of shifts.

Sandra scanned them briefly. 'I don't understand.'

'Compare the dates of David's work pattern, the dates highlighted, with the dates of these huge payments into Martinez account. You'll notice they're very close to one another. The payments were made just days after David's shift changes when Martinez yacht sailed into Boston.'

'Money laundering?' asked Sandra.

'Money laundering! It's my guess that the outward sailings consisted of drugs. The inbound journeys back to Boston contained the actual cash paid for the drugs. That's where David came in. Martinez would have carried out checks on David, found out what his job was and allowed him to slip deeper and deeper into debt so they had a hold over him. He would have been told to be on duty whenever they planned one of their voyages to allow them to go unhindered.'

'And once he decided to go to the police, they murdered him. Poor David, if only he'd said something earlier,' said Sandra.

'I'm sorry,' said Frank, 'of course, this is just a theory at the moment, but I think you'll agree, the evidence seems pretty strong.'

'How did you get hold of this information anyway?' asked Sandra.

'From one of David's colleagues who wanted to help. You may even know him, Alec Mundy.'

'Alec, yes, I know him well. They were good friends as well as colleagues. I hope he doesn't get into trouble for giving you this.'

'Talking of which, what about you, Sandra?'

'Oh, don't worry about me.'

'But I do.'

'Really Frank, I'll be fine. So, where do we go from here?'

'*We* are not going anywhere, from here on in, I go it alone. It could be dangerous, these people don't play nice,' said Frank earnestly.

'I can't let you do that. I want to help – I need to help.'

'We'll see, but right now, I need to get more proof, and that's not going to be easy. For now, just go home and take care of yourself – I'll be in touch. And if you're ever afraid, just call me and the police straight away.'

'The police? They're a joke. They don't seem interested in David's murder at all. It seems to me, you're the only one who is, Frank.'

'Can I keep this for now?' Frank said, gesturing to the ejected memory stick.

'Yes, of course,' Sandra said, getting up from the chair.

'Thanks. Now let me know when you're home safely, will you?'

'Yes, I'll do that, Frank. And thank you,' she said, squeezing his hand.

Frank watched as she got in her car and drove off. He returned to his office and began to put the papers provided by Alec Mundy back into the filing cabinet, switched off his PC and stuffed the memory stick in the pocket of his pants.

He was about to lock his office and go up to his apartment when from nowhere, it seemed, Martinez and his gorilla approached from behind. Bobby pushed Frank back into his office. Martinez and Bobby followed as Frank stumbled to the floor.

'I see you're keeping busy Mr Doyle, seeing clients at this time of night. Or was it Miss Gray you were having such a long tête-à-tête with?'

'None of your business, Martinez,' said Frank, lifting himself up from the floor, 'now get out of my office.'

'Hmm, take a seat, Mr Doyle.'

'I think I'll stand again if it's all the same to you.'

'Bobby!' Martinez gestured with a wave of his finger to the client's chair while he sat in Franks, putting his feet up on the desk. Bobby stood behind Frank, threateningly.

'Close the blinds, Bobby, there's a good man,' said Martinez, grinning. Bobby obeyed, as he always did. 'There, that's better, isn't it?' said Martinez.

'I suppose you're here to give me another beating, is that it?' said Frank, coolly.

'Of course not, Frank. Oh, you don't mind if I call you Frank, do you?'

'Only my friends and family call me Frank, and you're neither.'

'Oh, that's a shame, Frank, because you see, I was thinking perhaps we *could* be friends.'

'Oh, Really?'

'Yes. Oh, I realise we got off to a bad start, but I have a business proposition for you. You see, I could use a man like you, Frank, and I reward my people very well, believe me. I'm sure you could earn a great deal more than you're earning now.'

'What kind of work would that be exactly?'

'Well, to start, I think general security at my casino. After that, who knows. The sky's the limit, Frank. What do you say?'

'I don't think so, do you?'

'I suggest very strongly that you do think about it.'

'I'd like some time.'

'Of course you would. I'll tell you what I'll do, Frank, I'll give you a whole 48 hours to think about it. Should you decide to take up my offer, then come along to the casino to talk over the details. You won't regret it, I promise you.'

'Okay, I'll think about it.'

'Excellent!' said Martinez, removing his feet from Frank's desk. He stood upright, he and Bobby approached the office door to leave. Standing in the doorway, he turned to Frank before he left. 'Just one other thing before I leave, if you're going to work for me, I need you to break ties with the young woman who just left your office – 48 hours, Frank.'

'And if I decide not to work for you?'

Martinez smiled wryly. 'You can't be that naïve, Frank.'

After Martinez and Bobby had left, Frank mopped the beads of perspiration from his forehead, took a bottle of bourbon from the bottom drawer of his filing cabinet and poured himself a large one in a tumbler.

Frank sat at his desk, considering the offer, taking the occasional swig of the liquor. Ten minutes later his cell phone rang, it was Sandra.

'Hi Frank, just to let you know, I've just got home,' she said.

'That's good,' said Frank sombrely.

'Anything wrong?' asked Sandra.

'Listen to me carefully, Sandra. I had a visit from Martinez and his gorilla just after you left…'

'Oh no, they didn't work you over again did they Frank?'

'No, nothing like that, but I'd feel happier if you moved back with your mother for a while.'

'Why? And what did Martinez want this time?'

'Don't concern yourself with that. Just trust me, it's for the best you move out. They're watching us.'

'Okay Frank, if you think I should.'

'I do. And one other thing, you'd better not come to my office again, at least not for a while.'

'If you say so, Frank, but will you be okay? I'm worried about you.'

'I'll be fine, don't worry about me. Goodnight, Sandra.'

Frank finished his bourbon in one large gulp, locked up his office and retired to his apartment. It was a long and sleepless night as he considered Martinez's offer.

Chapter Fifteen

Thirty-six hours passed since Hugo Martinez's visit. Frank, after much soul-seeking, decided to take up his offer and called the casino. Connected to a young woman at a switchboard, he asked to speak to Martinez and gave his name to the operator. It was clear that not anyone would be connected to Martinez unless it was someone *he* wished to speak to. There was a long pause as the operator put him on hold. Eventually, she came back on the line and said she was putting him through.

'Frank, how nice to hear from you,' said Martinez, his phone on speaker.

'Good morning Mr Martinez,' said Frank, through gritted teeth.

'Have you thought about my offer?'

'Yes, I have, and I came to the conclusion that you're right, what I do is a mug's game.'

'So, you've decided to join me and my team. I can't tell you how pleased I am.'

'Well, I'd like to know what you're offering before I fully decide.'

'I take it you're talking about money. Well let's see. How does $500 a week sound? Of course, that's just for starters you understand, after a satisfactory trial period your earnings, well, let's say will increase substantially.'

'That sounds okay to me,' said Frank.

'Excellent! When can you start?'

'Straight away I guess.'

'Good, I was hoping you'd say that. Could you come to my office at 5pm and Bobby will get you familiarised with your duties.'

'Okay, I'll see you then.'

'I look forward to it,' said Martinez, and then hung up. His thin smile disappeared and with a serious tone, he turned to Bobby, his right-hand man who had been listening with interest. 'Keep an eye on him, watch every move he makes.'

'Will do boss,' said Bobby, his voice low, emotionless.

Being pleasant to Martinez over the phone had left a bad taste in Frank's mouth. He wondered what his next move might be once he was working for him. It wouldn't be easy and he only intended to be in his employ for a matter of days. It was his hope that during that time he could somehow gather intelligence on his operation, enough to put him away for a long time. Just how he could achieve that, however, he wasn't sure.

Furthermore, he had no intention of failing his clients, he had to consider his reputation as a man who could be relied on.

Around eighteen hours before, Sandra had called the bank where she worked and left a message with the switchboard operator to pass on to her boss, Karen, that she was taking a few days leave. She had taken Frank's advice and gone to her mothers about an hour's drive from Boston city. Arrangements for David's funeral had been made and it was to take place the following day. It would mean travelling back to the city briefly. Family, friends and colleagues had been informed; she also left a message on Frank's voicemail.

Sandra's mother, Pru, had always liked David and treated him like the son she'd never had. She was naturally extremely sad about his death, particularly the nature of it and had great sympathy for her daughter, yet since the revelation of his gambling and the lie he had been living, she was secretly grateful the two had never actually got around to getting married.

'All I'm saying dear is, how will you manage to pay the rent on your apartment now that you only have your income to rely on?' said Pru, as she made them both some coffee.

'Oh mother, do stop fussing. I can't think about that at the moment,' said Sandra, seating herself at the kitchen table. Big and rambling, the house had been the one which Sandra had grown up in. Her father had passed away some four years earlier, yet her mother insisted she could still manage without moving to a smaller, more manageable property. Out of town, it was also fairly isolated.

'Well, someone has to think of these things. You could always move back here with me until you…'

'Find someone else? Is that what you were going to say mother?'

'What I was going to say, that is, before you interrupted me, was, until you could find a flatmate to share the cost. Is that so terrible a thing to say?'

Sandra drew the mug of coffee to her lips. 'No, it isn't, I just can't think about that sort of thing at the moment, I will, but not until after David's funeral. I'm sorry for snapping, mom.'

'It's alright dear, I understand. But you can't blame me for worrying about you.'

'I know.' Sandra said, reaching across the table and gently squeezing her mother's hand. She knew deep down that Pru meant well.

Their coffee break was interrupted by a call on Sandra's cell phone. It was her boss.

'Hello, Sandra.' Her voice sounded more stern than usual.

'Hi Karen, how are things?' Sandra said, getting up from her chair and pacing the floor as she spoke.

'Fine, but we need to talk as soon as you return to work, Sandra.'

'Okay, is something wrong?'

'When do you expect to be back?'

'Well, as you know, it's David's funeral tomorrow. I'm hoping to be back in the office a day, or maybe two at the most after that. Is that okay?'

'Yes, that's fine,' Karen said, her voice still firm. 'And I'm very sorry, but I won't be able to make it to the funeral tomorrow.'

'No problem. I understand.'

'Alright, I'll see you in a few days,' Karen said, before hanging up abruptly.

'Your office?' asked Pru, inquisitively.

'Yes.'

'Everything okay? You look worried.'

'Everything's fine, just fine,' Sandra said, returning to her coffee.

'I hope so,' said Pru, 'the last thing you need right now is trouble at work.'

'Mom! I just said there's nothing wrong. She simply wanted to know when I'd be returning to work, that's all.'

'I see dear. More coffee?'

'Not for me, thanks. I'd better check on my clothes for tomorrow.'

'Of course. You'd better make sure you have a dark coat and umbrella as well; I believe rain is forecast.'

'Yes, I know. Why does it always seem to rain for funerals?'

'It poured down for your father's. Do you remember?'

'Yes, of course, how could I forget?'

Sandra went to her old room, took a black trouser suit and white shirt from the closet which she had brought from her apartment. It needed an iron running over it, she would do that later, right now she was worried about her position at the bank. There was little doubt in her mind why Karen was eager to speak to her on her return to the office.

Hacking into Martinez's account was a serious matter, she had always known that. Now she wondered if it had been worth risking her career for. Unsure how she would cope if she was to lose her job as well as David, she sat on the bed and for the first time in days and quietly wept.

Chapter Sixteen

It was 5pm sharp when Frank arrived at the casino. He was met inside the main doors by Bobby Downes who was awaiting his arrival. He stood menacingly, legs apart, arms folded, and he looked less than pleased to see Frank.

'Follow me,' he said sternly.

They entered the lift and took the short journey to Martinez's office suite, standing next to one another in silence. The man towered over Frank, motionless, his eyes fixed unblinkingly at the lift door in front of him. The door opened and he ushered Frank into the large open office.

'Mr Doyle for you boss,' said Bobby.

'Frank, come in and take a seat my friend,' said Martinez, gesturing to a chair facing his desk. He got up from his sumptuous leather office chair and reached out to shake Frank's hand. Frank didn't like doing it one little bit, but he shook his hand anyway and forced a smile. 'I can't tell you how much it gladdens my heart that you've decided to work for me,' he added.

'Pleased to be here,' said Frank.

'Drink?' asked Martinez.

'Don't mind if I do.'

'You look like a bourbon man to me, am I right?'

'Bourbon will do just fine, thanks.'

Martinez went to his drink cabinet and poured generously. 'We will need to get a black tux and pants for you, I'm sure we'll have some that'll fit you. We'll deal with that later, but for now, Bobby will show you around and tell you what your duties will consist of, that is of course, after we've finished our drink together. Cheers my friend,' he said, raising his glass.

'Cheers,' Frank replied. 'There is just one thing, I'm afraid I won't be able to work tomorrow, I have to attend a funeral.'

'Oh, I'm sorry to hear that, Frank. Someone close?' asked Martinez, glancing at Bobby.

'No, a brief acquaintance, but I feel I should attend all the same.'

'Of course,' said Martinez, 'there's absolutely no rush for you to start work. Simply knowing you're on-board is good enough for me, Frank.'

'I can start the day after tomorrow, no problem,' said Frank.

'That's just fine,' said Martinez with a broad smile. 'Here's to a long and fruitful relationship,' he said, raising his glass once again.

Frank raised his glass and took a long gulp of his bourbon, finishing it off.

'Okay, well, Bobby will now take you downstairs and show you the ropes and get you fitted up with a suit. I look forward to seeing you in a couple of days then Frank.' He got up from behind his desk and shook Frank's hand once again. 'And if you have any questions, Bobby will be only too pleased to answer them for you. Well goodnight, Frank.'

'Goodnight, and, uh, thanks for the opportunity,' Frank said, almost choking on the words.

'My pleasure, Frank. I need good men like you.'

Frank and Bobby stepped into the elevator. Martinez still had a broad smile on his face as the doors closed just before the two descended to the ground floor. As they stepped out, Bobby stopped in his tracks and turned to Frank.

'Let's get one thing straight. I don't like you and I don't trust you, but the boss has taken to you and what the boss says – goes, understand?'

'Sure, that all seems pretty clear. And for what it's worth, I don't like you either.'

There was a pause before, uncharacteristically, Bobby laughed aloud. 'You've got guts – I'll say that for you.'

'Well, I'm glad we got that out in the open,' said Frank, 'maybe now, you can show me what I have to do around here.'

'There's not much to it, you just keep your eyes open for any trouble. You'll also be given an earpiece which the boss will use to talk to you.'

Bobby led Frank to a door marked private, he tapped in a code on the door entry pad. A young woman sat at a desk that had a number of CCTV monitors on it, they were all trained on all areas around the roulette and blackjack tables. Frank said, 'Hi,' and she smiled timidly.

'If there's any sign of cheating, Julie will let the boss know and he'll speak to you on your earpiece, you quietly ask the person for a word and then take him or her upstairs – clear?'

'Seems pretty straightforward,' said Frank.

'That's about all there is to it. Now, come with me and we'll find you some clothes. After that, you can go home and report to me in a couple of days in time for your first shift at 6pm. Your shift will end at 2am, okay.'

'Okay, fine,' said Frank.

The entire introduction had only taken an hour and thirty minutes, and now Frank was driving homeward bound with his black suit draped on the rear seat. It was 6.30pm, still early, so he decided to get a drink and something to eat at a diner just a short walk from his apartment.

He had hated being agreeable with Martinez and his heavy, but it was a necessary evil. It was the only way he could begin to gain their trust. Whether it would work or not, he wasn't sure, but he knew he had to try if he was to discover more about Martinez's operation and find proof that he was directly linked to David Ryan's murder.

He parked his car and walked to the diner, it was convenient and the food wasn't bad either, he used it quite frequently.

'Hi Frank,' said a waitress.

'Hi Marlene,' he said, seating himself in a booth.

He had already decided what he wanted as she approached, it was the same as he always ordered, a sixteen-ounce steak and a side order of salad along with a cold beer.

'The usual, Frank?'

'You got it,' said Frank.

'Coming right up, honey,' said Marlene. 'Must be a week since I last saw you last, where have you been, Frank?'

'Yeah, I've been a little tied up during the last few days.'

'Good to see you anyway. I'll just see to your order, honey. Shouldn't be too long.'

As he waited, he took his cell-phone and called Sandra. She answered immediately.

'Hi Frank,' she said, her voice sorrowful.

'Hi Sandra. You okay?'

'No, not really, Frank.'

'That's understandable. You're thinking about tomorrow?'

'Yes, that, and my future.'

'You'll be okay, but it'll take time. Believe me, I know.'

'Yes, I know, but there's something else. My boss called me today, I think I'm in danger of losing my job.'

'Has this anything to do with the Martinez account you looked into?'

'I think so, it couldn't be anything else.'

'Oh, Jesus, I should never have allowed you to go ahead with it,' said Frank.

'It's not your fault, Frank. It was my decision and mine alone. I guess I'll just have to pay the price. I knew the risk.'

'Look, try not to worry. I take it you're still at your mother's?'

'Yes.'

'Good. I'll see you tomorrow. Try to get a good night's sleep.'

'I'll try. Okay, see you tomorrow, Frank. Bye.'

The waitress brought Frank's beer to his booth. 'You okay, Frank? You look miles away.'

'Yeah, I'm fine, Marlene. Just a little tired.

'Well, don't you worry, your food will be along shortly, honey,' she said, cheerfully patting his broad shoulder.

By the time his steak arrived, Frank had lost his appetite and left most of it uneaten. He felt a deep guilt about the possibility of Sandra losing her job because of his determination to bring Martinez and his man to justice. He even began to doubt if he was on the right track. What if he was wrong, and Martinez had nothing to do with David Ryan's murder? The thought of it brought him down. He paid his tab and walked back to his apartment, but first checked his mail and answering machine for messages in his ground floor office.

His mail consisted of nothing important. He pressed play on the flashing answering machine, there were two enquiries for his services, both callers requesting him to call them back to arrange appointments to see him. He felt he could still keep his business rolling along whilst in the employ of Martinez. It would mean working during part of the day for himself, grabbing an hour or so sleep, then going to the casino in the evenings, but he didn't mind.

He went upstairs to his apartment, picked out a white shirt, black tie and shone a pair of black shoes in readiness for the funeral the next day. The dark grey suit he was already wearing would have to do. His long black overcoat would virtually cover it in any case, he thought. Frank switched on the Calm Radio station, hung up his suit and laid back on his sofa in his shorts. He was asleep before the first tune ended.

Chapter Seventeen

Frank woke with a jolt. He had slept through the whole night on his sofa. The radio was still playing non-stop soothing music. Bleary-eyed, he glanced at his watch, it was 7.30am. Yawning, he sat upright and stretched his arms. Raising himself, he walked over to the window and opened the blinds. As had been predicted, it was a grey, gloomy day and raining steadily.

He grabbed a bathrobe from his bedroom and made his way to the kitchen, made himself a cup of instant coffee and poured some cornflakes into a bowl along with a splash of milk. Sipping his coffee, he gradually felt more revived and ready to face the day, a second cup would complete the job.

The funeral was to be at 3.30pm at The Forest Hill's Cemetery in Boston. As Frank understood it, David had lost both his parents at a young age but had a brother and several cousins. All were spread widely across the country, his brother would, of course be attending, according to Sandra. His cousins, however, were less likely to make it, due to the distance involved.

Nevertheless, he had, by all accounts, a wide group of friends and colleagues who thought a great deal of him, they would undoubtedly be there to say goodbye, he thought.

His mind wandered to what Sandra had told him the evening before, and it still troubled him greatly. He felt responsible for her being in trouble with the bank where she worked. It seemed a hopeless state of affairs and *he* was powerless to do anything about it. He almost wished he had not been at O'Malley's on that fateful night. The weather suited his mood, the rain was becoming heavier.

Amid a sea of black umbrellas and following a short graveside service, Sandra picked up a handful of moist earth and tossed it onto David's coffin below and turned to her mother who took her arm. Others followed, including Frank, in gently throwing some earth into the grave. Frank noticed that, standing back from the grave, was John McKay. He was keeping a low profile, unsure whether a representative of the Boston police department would be entirely welcome.

Sandra walked over to Frank with her mother and David's brother. 'Hi Frank,' she said, almost shouting to be heard over the rain beating down on her umbrella. 'Can I introduce you to my mother and this is David's brother, Harry.'

'I'm very pleased to meet you both. I wish it were under happier circumstances. Please accept my condolences,' he said, turning to David's brother.

'Thank you,' said Harry, 'how did you know David?'

Sandra interjected. 'Frank's a private investigator. He found David that night and he's kindly looking into his murder.'

'I see, Mr?'

'Doyle. Pleased to meet you.'

'I'm sorry, Mr Doyle, I had no idea that Sandra had hired a private investigator.'

'Well, not hired exactly,' said Frank.

'And how's your investigation going, Mr Doyle?' Pru interrupted.

'It's a little early to say at the moment, Mrs Gray, but I'm hopeful,' said Frank, reassuringly.

'Well, I'm glad we have you on our side, Mr Doyle,' said Harry, 'the police seem to think it's nothing more than a waste of their time.'

'Rest assured; I'll do everything I can.'

'I know it's a long way for you to travel, but will you come back to my mother's house for some refreshments?' said Sandra.

'Thank you, Sandra, but I'm afraid I can't, I'm sorry.'

'I understand, that's okay.'

'Do you think I could I have a quick word?' asked Frank.

'Of course, I won't be a moment, mom.' They wandered a few yards to be in private.

'It's about what you told me last night,' said Frank in a low voice, 'I'm worried about you. Do you really think you may lose your job?'

'Frank, there's no need for you to worry, it's not your responsibility.'

'But do you?'

'Well, bank's do tend to take a dim view of their staff hacking into accounts which have nothing to do with them. I'd say the chances are pretty high.'

'I feel terrible, I should never have…'

'Frank, there's no need, there is absolutely no way it's your fault. I knew what I was doing,' she said, stoically.

'Yes, but…'

'No but's, Frank, it was my choice. I'll be okay,' she said, still having to raise her voice to be heard over the deluge. 'I'd better get back to the others, Frank. I'll speak to you soon, okay.'

The many people attending the funeral were now dispersing to escape the rain, all paying their respects to Sandra before leaving. Frank noticed John McKay standing on his own, getting soaked to the skin by the graveside. McKay beckoned Frank over to him.

'John, here, get under,' said Frank, offering to share his umbrella.

'I wouldn't worry too much about that, I couldn't get any wetter if I tried,' John replied, miserably.

'I'm surprised to see you here. Were you sent by the department?'

'No, I wasn't sent. I just felt I should pay my respects. I'd would say I'm surprised to see you too – but I'm not. You still pursuing this case, Frank?'

'I won't lie to you, John, yeah, I'm still looking into it.'

'Don't know how many times I have to say it, Frank, why don't you leave it alone?'

'Why are you so eager for me to drop it, John?'

'Argh, forget it. I can see I'm not gonna change your mind. Do what the hell you like. See you around, Frank, you stubborn bastard.'

'I remember when you used to be a stubborn bastard as well. See you around, John.'

They parted ways and both ran to their respective vehicles. Frank unlocked his door and shook the water from his umbrella before seating himself in his car. Just as he was about to switch on the ignition, there was a loud banging on the driver's window, he looked up to see it was a very soggy Alec Mundy. Frank wound the window down a little.

'Get in,' said Frank, gesturing to the passenger seat.

Alec rushed round and got in the vehicle. 'Sorry, Frank, I'm a little wet, as you can see.'

'Don't worry about, so am I. What can I do for you, Alec?'

'I was just wondering how the investigation was going?'

'Well, I'm still trying to gather more information on Martinez. That's about all I can say at the moment,' said Frank.

'Is there anything else I can do to help?' asked, Alec.

'It's good of you to offer, but I don't see that there's anything at this time. Has Martinez yacht come in yet?'

'Not yet. I'd say it's overdue.'

'Well maybe there is something you could do. Could you give me a call when it *does* appear?' asked Frank.

'Sure, no problem,' said Alec, eager to help in any way he could.

'That'd be great, thanks Alec.'

'How do you think Sandra is holding up?' asked Alec.

'I think she's putting on a very brave face at the moment. But it's early days, I think she'll be okay.'

'Yeah, I'm sure you're right, she's pretty tough.'

'Anyway, Alec, I have to be somewhere, so…'

'Yeah, sure thing. And I'll let you know about Martinez's yacht, okay. Bye Frank.'

Frank glanced at his watch; it was around 4.30pm. He was to start his first shift at 6pm, by reporting to Bobby. He would need to arrive a little earlier, he imagined, so he drove at a steady pace in order to get back to his place and change clothes.

It had stopped raining when he arrived at Hugo's casino. Frank left his vehicle, checked his bow tie and the rather tightly fitting suit that had been supplied. He was in good time, so he took a few puffs on a cigar before extinguishing it and saving the rest until 2am when he finished his shift. He walked in to the casino's lobby, to be met by Bobby, who looked Frank up and down for a moment.

'You'll do,' said Bobby. 'Follow me.'

Frank dutifully followed into the main room where the serious gambling took place. 'Okay, just a couple of things, no drinking, except coffee or soda when you take your break, no smoking, and no socializing with the clients – understood?' said Bobby.

'Yeah, I understand,' said Frank.

'Okay, here's your earpiece. Put it in, listen out for anything from the boss and keep your eyes on the tables. That's all you have to do.'

It was fairly boring work, yet in some ways very similar to his real job, observing people, looking out for trouble. He was three hours into his shift, the young waiter whom he'd met a few nights earlier, recognised Frank and gave a sideways glance as he passed by.

His earpiece had so far been quiet, but now Martinez's voice came through it. 'Good-evening Frank, settling in I hope. I've been watching you and you're doing just fine. Bobby will be relieving you shortly, so you can take a break.' Frank automatically said, 'Thanks,' before remembering it was a one-way conversation.

After Bobby took over and directed him to a small staff only room, Frank made his way there, keeping an eye open for any other rooms that were out of bounds to the public. On his way to the staff room, he noticed another door with a sign stating "Staff Only," he peered inside, it was the cleaner's room. Perhaps an ideal place to hide after his shift. But not tonight, he thought.

'Find anything interesting?' said Bobby, appearing, it seemed from nowhere.

'Sorry, wrong door,' said Frank.

'Next door along,' said Bobby, suspiciously.

'My mistake,' said Frank, swiftly moving on. He reached the staff room and looked back. Bobby was still watching him. 'This one, I take it?' Frank said, grabbing the door handle. Bobby simply nodded and waited until Frank had entered the room before returning to the casino floor.

Frank was alone in the room. A pot of coffee was being kept hot, he poured himself a cup and pondered how he could gain access to Martinez's office after the casino closed for the night. The cleaner's room could have been an ideal place to hide, but not now he had been caught snooping. He was painfully aware that Martinez had offered him the job so that he could keep an eye on him, at least for some of the time. It was a matter of Martinez keeping his enemy close, no matter how pleasant he was appearing to be. Frank wasn't fooled for a moment about that, but then again, he thought, neither was Martinez fooled about him accepting the job. They both knew the score. It was simply a matter of who could be the smartest that would decide the outcome. Martinez may be a crook and perhaps a murderer, but stupid he isn't, thought Frank.

The end of Frank's shift finally arrived, it had been a long and fruitless evening. The one thing he had learned was that he was being watched very carefully. He went to his car and looked up at the three-storey building. He knew that Martinez's office was on the first floor and could only assume that perhaps the second floor was his penthouse suite. It was going to be a difficult task to gain access to the office undetected. It was perhaps time to re-think his strategy.

Chapter Eighteen

Two days after David Ryan's funeral, Sandra could stand the uncertainty no longer and decided to return to the bank. Her expectations of keeping her job, she thought, were not good. What she had done was a serious offence, she fully expected to be fired on the spot, if not arrested. Her mother knew she was troubled about her job, but Sandra had kept the truth from her. Now though, it may all come out in the open. Pru would be devastated.

She was not expecting a welcoming committee, but was shocked, when entering the bank, a security guard approached and took her by the arm.

'I'm very sorry, Miss Gray, but I have orders to take you straight up to the CEO's office.'

Sandra bit her bottom lip but somehow held back the tears. She composed herself as best she could. 'Okay,' she said calmly, 'but do you think you could release my arm, Stan?'

The guard nodded. 'Sure. I'd like you to know I'm very sorry about this,' he said, sympathetically. 'I'm sure there's some misunderstanding that can be sorted out.'

'Thanks, but I don't think so,' she said, resignedly, as they approached the elevator. They stepped inside and the guard pressed the button for the top floor. The journey took only moments, yet it seemed like forever to Sandra. Her heart was in her mouth as they passed by her office and on to Karen's next door. Karen's secretary scowled at Sandra as she and the guard entered. She said nothing, simply buzzed Karen on the intercom and informed her of Sandra's arrival.

'Thank you, send her in and tell Stan he can return to his duties,' said Karen, sternly. Sandra entered, her heart beating out of her chest.

'So, you've turned up to face the music. I don't think I need to ask if you know what this is all about, do I?'

'No.'

'Sit down,' said Karen, her voice softening slightly. 'We've known one another for a long time and I've always trusted you implicitly. So my question is this – Why?'

'It's a long story, Karen, I can explain,' said Sandra timidly.

'Well, I'm listening.'

Sandra paused. 'Actually, I'm not sure I can explain. It'll sound ridiculous.'

'I don't care how ridiculous it sounds; I want to know. You do realize how serious an offence this is?'

'Yes, I do.'

'Come on, Sandra, tell me. You'll feel better for it, believe me. Why the Martinez account?'

'I – I can't,' said Sandra, beginning to weep.

Karen passed her a box of tissues from her desk and rubbed her forehead in frustration. 'Look, I know what you've been going through recently, but you have to tell me what's going on. Tell me you're having a breakdown or something – anything. Just talk to me.'

'Maybe I am having a breakdown,' said Sandra, composing herself a little.

Karen looked at Sandra thoughtfully. Realistically, that explanation was never going to wash with her. 'Yes, maybe you are, but that doesn't explain why you specifically hacked into the Martinez account, does it?'

'You really will think I'm mad if I told you the truth.'

'Try me?'

'I think Martinez had something to do with David's death. I was trying to find out more about him. Well, there it is! There's nothing else to say.'

'I see. And what makes you think that, Sandra?'

'I've been working with a private investigator. He's convinced Martinez was directly involved in David's murder.'

'I still don't see why hacking into his personal account would help.'

'It's far too complicated to explain, Karen.'

'Is that your last word?'

'What are you going to do?' asked Sandra, nervously.

'I'm sorry, Sandra, but I don't see that you're leaving me any other choice but to let you go. If I can't trust you and you won't explain your actions fully, then…'

'But what if I could prove to you that…'

'I'm very sorry, Sandra, I really am. My secretary will escort you to your office to clear your desk.'

'But Karen, you can't, I thought we were friends.'

'I'm sorry.' Karen asked her secretary to come into her office. 'Please take Miss Gray to her old office to clear her desk, then escort her off the premises. Before you go Sandra, I'll take your office key and identity badge, please.'

'Please don't do this, Karen,' pleaded Sandra.

'Goodbye, Sandra,' said Karen coldly.

The mean-spirited secretary looked on gleefully. 'Come with me,' she said, grabbing Sandra's arm. Sandra shook her off. 'Don't you touch me,' she said, angrily, the young woman simply sneered at her.

Sandra collected her personal belongings under the watchful eye of Karen's secretary, her framed diplomas, a photograph of David and other assorted items and, boxed them and left the office, making her way to the elevator with the unpleasant woman. Downstairs, she said goodbye to the much kinder security guard and left the premises for good. How was she going to tell her mother she had been fired, and explain the circumstances behind it? Her career had been so promising, she'd never imagined for one moment that she would be leaving the bank under such a cloud.

Sandra put her box of belongings in the trunk. Losing her job, as well as David was too much for her, she sat at the steering wheel and wept, she could feel her whole life crumbling before her. She remained seated behind the wheel for some several minutes, the reality of her situation truly sinking in. Would she, on top of everything else, lose her apartment and be forced to live with her mother again. Not that she didn't love her dearly, but the strain of living together would be challenging. There was so much to consider, her mind was in a spin.

Right now, all Sandra wanted was a sympathetic ear. She could think of no one better than Frank and called his cell phone.

'Frank Doyle,' he answered.

'Frank, it's Sandra,' she said, still sobbing a little.

'Sandra, you okay? You sound upset.'

'No, I'm not okay, Frank, I'm afraid. Do you think I could meet you to talk?'

'Of course, when?'

'As soon as possible.'

'Sure, but not at my place. I'm still not sure if I'm being watched or not. There's a diner just along the street from me, Martha's Kitchen. We could meet there. Has something happened?'

'Yes, I'll tell you about it when I see you. Can I meet you in say, thirty-minutes?'

'That's just fine. I'll meet you there.'

Frank took a slow stroll down to the diner, arriving early to secure a quiet booth. The rain had lessened from the day before, yet the sky was ominously dark. Martha's Kitchen always had a pleasant atmosphere and was almost always busy. However, he found a booth that would afford them a degree of privacy. He didn't have to wait too long before Sandra arrived. Frank spotted her scanning the booths for him. He raised his hand to attract her attention and she walked solemnly over to him.

'Take a seat, Sandra,' he said. She looked pale and defeated as she sat opposite him. 'What's upsetting you so badly?' asked Frank, 'tell me what's happened.'

'Oh Frank,' she said, beginning to cry again.

Frank took out a clean handkerchief from his breast pocket and handed it to her. 'Take your time, honey.'

'What can I get you folks?' asked a waitress.

'Just coffee,' said Frank.

'Coming right up.'

After the waitress had rushed off, Sandra finally managed to find her voice. 'I've just been to the bank, my boss fired me. I don't know what to do, Frank.'

'Oh Jesus, I'm so sorry, Sandra. I take it this has something to do with the Martinez account.'

'Yes, of course.'

'This is my fault. No matter how much you deny it, it *is* my fault,' said Frank, angry with himself.

'No Frank, I won't have you saying that. It's not true. I told you before, I knew what I was doing – or at least, I thought I did. Now though…'

'With your qualifications, you'll find another job, I'm sure of it,' said Frank.

'I don't think any bank will touch me now, Frank. Maybe we should drop this whole thing.'

'Is that what you want?' asked Frank as the coffee arrived.

'I don't know,' she said, taking a sip of her coffee. 'Maybe it would be for the best. I've lost my job; you've been worked over. I'm not sure about anything anymore, Frank.'

'What if I went to speak to your boss, told her it was me that put you up to it? Do you think it might help to get your job back?'

'I doubt it very much. I want to thank you for everything, Frank, but I think it's time to call it a day.'

'Okay, I won't involve you anymore, but let's stay in touch, okay.'

'Of course we will. I could use a friend right now, Frank.'

Chapter Nineteen

Frank walked back home in a sombre mood. He went straight into his office before going upstairs to his apartment. He needed to catch up with prospective clients who had left messages for him and to check his mail. Yet all the time, he couldn't get Sandra's situation out of his mind – if only there was a way he could help her, he thought.

He was due to report for his shift at Hugo's Casino at 6pm again that evening. Was it all a waste of time? He wasn't sure. But the truth of the matter was that he couldn't see a way forward with his investigation by working for Martinez. The security, it seemed, was too tight. The man's office, and presumably his penthouse suite were both protected like a fortress. At the moment, it all seemed quite hopeless.

In the unlikely event that he could gain access to Martinez's office, what would he find? The chances are, he thought, that there would be nothing incriminating. A murderous crook he may be, but he certainly wasn't stupid.

Frank spent an hour or so contacting his prospective clients and arranging appointments for them at his office. He also did a background check on Bobby Downes to find his address for his Mr Robinson, he'd not had a chance to do so until now. The background check also revealed that the man had past criminal convictions for assault. It was no surprise. Frank emailed his address to Mr Robinson to pass onto his lawyer in case he decided to pursue divorce proceedings against his wife.

All of this had been a welcome distraction from his thoughts about Sandra. He decided to have lunch and catch a little sleep before his shift at the casino. He wasn't sure how long he could keep this up, working a long shift for Martinez at night and also keeping his business running smoothly by day. He managed to grab around an hour of sleep, but it was not a sound sleep.

'Mr Martinez would like to see you before you start work,' said Bobby, as Frank arrived at the casino. Bobby Downes voice, as was usual, had an air of menace about it.

'Oh, okay,' said Frank, pensively.

'I'll take you up.'

'Sure,' said Frank.

As before, the journey up to the office was silent. Frank wondered what was in store for him. As far as he was aware, he had done nothing wrong.

'Frank, come in,' said Martinez, cheerfully, as the elevator door opened. 'Come and take a seat.'

'Thank you,' said Frank.

'I would offer you a drink,' said Martinez, 'but you're on duty, so…'

'Yes, of course,' said Frank, coolly.

'So, Frank, how was your first night?'

'It was fine. If I'm honest, I didn't have to do much, there was no trouble.'

'Yes, I know,' said Martinez, getting up from his chair and pacing the floor. 'You see, I know everything that goes on out on the floor. You'll find that last night was a typical night at my casino, Frank. We hardly ever have any trouble from our clients. They treat my place with respect, you see.'

'I understand.' Frank said, wondering where the line of conversation was leading to.

'And of course, that also applies to my staff,' Martinez said, placing his hands on the back of Frank's chair, gently rocking it. 'If my staff respect me, then I respect them, you understand?' Frank didn't flinch.

'Yeah, I understand.'

'So, no more snooping around, okay Frank,' Martinez said, his voice changing to a less friendly style.

'Snooping? I haven't been snooping,' said Frank, 'why would I be snooping?'

'I can't imagine. Unless, of course, you're still determined to continue your mindless investigation into me. Could that possibly be the case, Frank?' said Martinez, returning to his office chair.

'No, I told you, I've had enough of all of that. I just want a quiet life.'

'But you are still running your business, aren't you?'

'For the time being, yes. I understood this was a trial period. What if it doesn't work out, I'd have nothing to live on.'

'Fair enough, Frank. Well, you'd better get to work now.'

'Okay, thanks.'

Frank made his way to the elevator, yet again closely escorted by Bobby. The door opened and Frank began to step inside.

'Oh, by the way, how was the funeral? Asked Martinez.

'Fine,' said Frank, guessing that someone had been watching him.

'That's good.' Frank heard Martinez say as the elevator door closed.

Once on the casino floor, Frank went to work once again. He shielded his mouth with his hand as he yawned widely, he had seven- and three-quarter hours to go before his shift ended. He felt so tired. Having had little sleep, he didn't know how he would manage to stay awake. There was very little stimulation, yet he was painfully aware that his every move was being observed on camera and by Bobby on the casino floor.

After a couple of hours, Bobby came to relieve him and told him to take a break. 'I'd keep an eye on that guy,' said Frank, pointing to a man in a smart, dark suit at one of the roulette tables, 'he seems to be on a winning streak and I think he's got a system going.'

'I wouldn't worry too much about him, he'll lose it all before the night's out. He always does,' said Bobby, 'but well done.'

Frank made his way to get some much-needed coffee. To a small degree, he felt he had ingratiated himself and perhaps gained some trust. Yet he felt it would take a good deal more to gain complete trust. That could possibly take months, months he didn't have to spare. It was obvious he was being watched, not only at the casino, but in his private life also. That much was clear from Martinez's reference to the funeral. He had been seen there, there was no doubt in Frank's mind about that.

After his coffee and a visit to the bathroom, Frank returned to the casino floor. He had only returned a few minutes when his cell phone rang. He wondered if it might be Sandra. He took the phone from his pocket to see that it was John McKay's number. He shifted uneasily on his feet as he answered, looking around the room for prying eyes.

'John, what can I do for you?'

'I need to see you, Frank.' His voice betrayed a nervousness.

'Okay, when?'

'Tonight?'

'Sorry buddy, I can't make it tonight.'

'Dammit. Tomorrow then?'

'Sure. What time and where?'

'How about eleven at Rowes Wharf Ferry?'

'Okay, I'll see you then. You okay? You sound…'

'Yeah yeah, I'm fine. I'll see you tomorrow, Frank.'

Frank's eyes scoured the room again as he replaced the phone in his pocket. McKay's voice had an urgency about it, something was troubling him and Frank felt guilty for not being able to meet him.

John McKay sat in a crowded bar; he had been drinking for some time. He preferred to be where there were plenty of people right now. He did not want to go home, yet knew he would have to when the bar closed for the night. He couldn't wait for the daylight and his meeting with Frank. There was no one else to turn to.

Chapter Twenty

After his lengthy shift at the casino, Frank hauled himself from his bed. He had slept a little better than the previous night at least, but working by day and also at the casino by night, he was not getting enough sleep.

It was 8.30am. He took a shower, got dressed and prepared a substantial breakfast of scrambled eggs and bacon with maple syrup and plenty of coffee. He slowly began to feel revived and able to face the day ahead. What would the day bring? He was still deeply concerned about Sandra and her situation; he would have to call her later to check on her. Yet now he had a new worry. When John McKay had called him, he had sounded scared. He'd given no clue about what was bothering him, yet Frank's instinct cried out to him that it was something to do with Martinez.

Come 10am, Frank drove to Rowes Wharf to meet John. Why he had chosen a ferry, for their meeting was beyond Frank's understanding, but if it made him feel better, it was fine by him. He arrived just around 10.40am and waited for John to arrive. It was a bright day, yet cool and breezy on the waterfront.

Frank glanced at his watch anxiously every couple of minutes. If they were to buy tickets for the 11am ferry, John had better arrive soon, he thought. By 10.50am, he was really beginning to think he'd been led on a wild goose chase, and five minutes later he was about to leave when John finally came into view, running towards Frank.

'We'd better hurry if we're going to get a ticket,' said Frank.

'Sorry I'm late, man, the traffic was hell,' said John with a pained expression.

'Didn't think you were going to make it. Come on.'

'You'll only just make it if you hurry,' said the woman in the ticket office, 'It's just about to leave.' The two ran for the ferry, only just making it in time. They found seats on the open, upper-deck after buying some coffee, the kind you get in paper cups with plastic lids.

'So, what's this all about, John?' asked Frank, pulling up his jacket collar to shield himself from the sea-breeze.

John hesitated for a moment before answering. 'It seems you were right all along, Frank. I've been doing some digging, and there's something rotten about the Ryan case.'

'I always knew you were a good cop. Go on,' said Frank.

'I've been asking questions in the department and my lieutenant got wind of it. He told me to lay off or hand in my badge. He virtually threatened me physically as well, told me that if I didn't shut my mouth…'

'What, what did he say?'

'He just pointed out that police officers sometimes met with nasty accidents. I think he and maybe even more senior officers may be on Martinez's payroll. That's what I believe. What other reason would he have in threatening me to lay off?' I don't mind telling you Frank, I'm scared.'

'Take it easy old friend.'

'That's easy to say, but I don't know what to do. I can't go to anyone about this.'

'What about internal affairs?'

'Right now, I don't trust anyone, Frank, yourself excepted. I'm taking a risk just meeting up with you. What do you think I should do?'

'Well, maybe you should lay off for the while. Let things cool down a little. If what you say is true, if they believe the heat is off, they'll leave you alone. That's my advice, for what it's worth, John.'

'Have you got anywhere with this, Frank?'

'I've got nothing concrete to prove Martinez had anything to do with Ryan's murder, but I do have some pretty interesting stuff on his financial affairs.'

'Like what?'

'Given what you've told me today, John, it's probably better you don't know. Just go to work and keep your head down. And you can call me at any time, you know that, don't you?'

'I appreciate that, Frank.'

Around an hour later, they parted company where they had begun their trip at Rowes Wharf. Each got into their vehicles and drove off in different directions. Frank was deeply concerned about his friend and the menacing threats he'd received from his lieutenant, but apart from the advice he had given, there seemed little else he could do. The case was proving to be a nightmare, the casualties were mounting-up. He truly *was* beginning to wish he had never been at O'Malley's bar that night.

On return to his office, Frank made himself a coffee, lit a long-awaited cigar and called Alec Mundy on his cell phone. Alec answered promptly.

'Hi Frank, I was just thinking about you.'

'Really? Why's that?'

'Well, as it goes, I've just been checking to see if Martinez's yacht had appeared yet.'

'And has it?'

'No. I don't understand it, it's taking much longer than usual.'

'Well, it seems you've answered the question I was calling about. I can't say I'm completely surprised, but I guess it'll have to come in some time, whether they have a stooge or not.'

'I guess so. Anyway, I'll keep you posted Frank.'

'Thanks Alec, appreciate it. Bye now.'

Frank considered the situation. If only he could set-up a sting operation. The question was, how? How could he gain the trust of Martinez? It seemed impossible. Martinez and his right-hand man were already distrustful of him and were watching his every move, it seemed. What could he do to get them to trust him without raising further suspicion? He wondered.

He took a beer from his small office fridge, poured it into a glass and puffed thoughtfully on his cigar. He was vaguely aware of the beginnings of a headache, which he rarely suffered from. It was probably due to a lack of sleep and the strain he was putting himself through, he thought.

Picking up his cell phone once again, he called Sandra's number.

'Hi Frank,' she sounded low.

'Hi Sandra, how are you?'

'Not good.'

'Are you still staying at your mother's?'

'No, I've moved back to my apartment, it seemed easier. At least that way my mom doesn't know I've lost my job. As far as she knows, I'm still going to the bank every day.'

'Any thoughts about what you'll do?'

'First of all, I need to get a flatmate if I'm going to stay here, then I'll have to start applying for jobs. Though God knows who'll take me on now.'

'I think you're a survivor, Sandra, something tells me you'll be fine. Besides, I've had a thought about a job, when this business with Martinez is over maybe we can discuss it.'

'Talking of which, why don't you drop it, Frank? Why do you insist on carrying on with this? You've done your best; you owe me nothing and you owe David nothing. Call it a day, Frank.'

'Well, as you know, I don't give up that easily. You take care of yourself, okay. I'll be in touch soon.'

Chapter Twenty-One

It was 8pm, and Frank was two hours into his shift at Hugo's Casino, he was feeling physically and mentally drained. For the past few days, he had been working virtually non-stop, he didn't know how much longer his body would tolerate this kind of treatment. A breakthrough in this case had to come soon, he thought, or was that simply wishful thinking, he had nothing to base it on.

The evening, as seemed usual, had been completely uneventful, Frank had found it difficult to stay awake. Yes, he was used to working long hours, but this lacked any stimulation whatsoever. What's more, it was getting him nowhere with his investigation – that being the prime reason he had taken the job in the first place.

Now his shift had finally ended, he made the decision to see Martinez before returning home. He had not seen Bobby the whole evening, which he thought was odd, but remembered the extension number for Martinez's office. He picked up a house phone and tapped out the three-digit number. To his initial surprize, Martinez knew it was him calling, but then turned and spotted one of the many security camera's trained on the location where he stood.

'Good-evening Frank,' said Martinez.

'Good-evening, or should I say, good-morning,' replied Frank.

Martinez laughed. 'What can I do for you, Frank?'

'I wondered if I could come up and see you. It won't take long.'

'Sounds ominous, Frank, but of course, come on up.'

A couple of minutes later, Frank arrived at Martinez's office and stepped out of the escalator.

'Do come in, Frank,' said Martinez, lounging on a sumptuous sofa with one of his girls. A heavy stood by the escalator door, yet there was still no sign of Bobby.

Martinez ordered the girl to leave, tapping her bottom as she stood up to go. 'Come and join me, Frank – drink?'

'No thanks, it's a little late for me.'

'As you wish, my friend. Now, what can I do for you?'

'Well, firstly, I'd like to thank you for the opportunity, but I've had a few days to think it over and I don't think it's for me,' said Frank.

Martinez's usual broad grin dropped. 'I see. I have to say, that is most disappointing, Frank.'

'It's just that I think I'm getting too old for these kinds of hours, and, well, to be honest, there isn't enough for me to do,' Frank said.

'Most disappointing indeed,' said Martinez, 'but if that's your final decision…'

'I'm afraid so. I'm very sorry,' said Frank, feigning an apology.

'So be it then,' said Martinez.

'I'll drop these clothes back tomorrow.'

'Keep them,' Martinez said, moving towards his desk. Frank's heart skipped a beat as he watched Martinez slowly open his desk drawer. He breathed again when he saw it was nothing more than a check book. 'Now,' said Martinez, picking up a pen, 'I think I'll pay you for the whole week – is that fair?'

'More than fair, that's very generous. Thank you.'

Martinez filled out the check and handed it to Frank. 'Well, I hope this can be a friendly parting of the ways, Frank.'

'Sure thing.'

Martinez's voice took on a serious tone. 'Do you mean that, Frank?'

'Of course.'

'Well let that be it then. But let me make myself clear, I don't want to hear from you or see you again – understood, Frank?'

'Yes, I understand. Message received loud and clear,' said Frank.

'Good, I'm glad we understand one another. Have a good life, Frank.'

'Thanks,' said Frank, as the escalator door began to close.

'I want to see Bobby as soon as he returns,' said Martinez to his other bodyguard.

'Sure boss.'

Frank tuned into CBS News Boston on his car radio, mainly to keep himself awake taking the drive home. It had seemed an extremely long evening and he was beyond tired. Martinez had agreed to him leaving his employ all too easily for Frank's liking. Yet he knew there were sinister undertones to their parting of the ways. Despite his now ex-bosses' words, he was certain that one way or another, he had not seen the last of Martinez.

For now though, he was looking forward to getting a good night's sleep, in the knowledge that tomorrow was his own. Apart from a couple of new clients that he had arranged to see at his office, the day was free, and he had already decided to take part of the day off.

The CBS news announcer hesitated for a moment before saying, *"And now some breaking news. Following a shoot-out at a domestic property in the Roxbury area of Boston, it is believed a police officer has been shot and killed in police cross-fire. Further details as we get them."* For a moment, what little hair Frank had, stood on end, but then it was an all-too-common event. He turned off the radio as he arrived outside his apartment.

Once inside, he made certain his apartment was secure, poured himself a glass of milk and went straight to bed.

He woke early the next morning, it was 6.30am, he had, for the first time in many nights, slept peacefully. He hadn't forgotten the promise he had made to himself about taking it easy that day, at least after he had seen his prospective clients during the morning. That was not to say Frank still didn't feel deeply saddened about Sandra, or indeed concern for his friend, John. He planned to call them both after his morning appointments.

Frank switched on the T.V in the kitchen to catch the news headlines as he made some coffee. The anchor-man read a few trivial pieces of news from his tele-prompter; his face then took on a serious appearance as he moved on to the next item. It was regarding the shoot-out the previous evening in Roxbury.

"And now we're going over live to Boston police headquarters where Police Chief, Steve Sanders is about to make a statement concerning the fatal shooting of a serving police officer late last night. Sally, over to you."

"Thank you, Bob. Yes, the Chief of Police is just appearing outside the headquarters now."

The substantial looking man stood on the steps of the Police H.Q surrounded by press and television cameras. Apart from the clicking of press photographer's cameras clicking, it went silent.

"Thank you, ladies and gentlemen. As you know, during the early hours of this morning at approximately 12.30am, police were called to an armed robbery in progress at an all-night store in the Roxbury district. This incident escalated into a siege and subsequent shoot-out. One of the two suspects was shot dead and it is with deep regret I have to inform you that a police officer was also shot and killed. His next of kin have been informed and I am now able to release the officer's name. Detective John McKay tragically died at the scene, and my thoughts are with his family."

Frank felt stunned.

The journalists and T.V reporters all bombarded him with questions about the incident. *"Can you confirm, that the police officer died as a result of police crossfire? Asked, Sally.*

"No questions at this time. There will of course be an inquiry." He turned and walked briskly up the steps and into the building.

Frank switched off the television. He sat at the kitchen table, bereft, and put his head in his hands and closed his eyes tightly to suppress the tears he felt coming. He had known John for many years; John had also, like Frank, moved from New York homicide to Boston. The grief would never leave Frank, neither would the guilt that he could have done more to protect him. Now his emotions turned to anger, he smashed his fist hard on the table.

Now it was time to get some real answers. Now it was personal.

Chapter Twenty-Two

Frank deferred his appointments for the day to a later date by email, he was too grief-stricken to talk. His thoughts of having a relaxing day head left him completely. He was now so angry, he wanted to do something positive, to ask questions and to bring John's murderer to justice. There was little doubt in his mind that it *was* murder, going by what John had told him only the day before. He was clearly living in fear for his life. Firstly though, he would pay his respects to John's widow, Mary. He knew her well and thought that she and her two teenage kids might appreciate a visit from a friendly face.

Having dressed in his dark grey suit, white shirt and black necktie, he drove out to the suburbs where they lived, it was a quarter after eleven. It was around a thirty-minute drive. Frank wasn't sure if he could find the right words of comfort, but then no words could possibly help so soon after his death. John was forty-five years old, his wife a few years younger, they had their whole lives ahead of them. He had only ten years to serve before his retirement.

Frank was still in a state of shock over his friend's death. The guilt of not doing more to protect him was overwhelming. During the early stages of his investigation into Ryan's murder, he had wondered if it was possible that John was somehow involved in a cover-up along with his lieutenant – another reason for guilt. He had seemed eager to keep Frank out of the loop which had made Frank suspicious. Now he would be kicking his own butt for ever thinking that. He had always been a good cop with never a hint of corruption or any wrong-doing.

It was still to be proved whether John's lieutenant was in Martinez's pocket. However, John wasn't a liar, nor was he inclined to exaggerate. It stood to reason that his threats to John meant something. Frank was determined to find out more.

Frank arrived at the leafy avenue to find a number of vehicles parked outside John's home, including a couple of black and white police vehicles. He left his car and apprehensively walked up the drive to the house. After ringing the doorbell, he was met by a woman he didn't know, she turned out to be Mary's sister, Beth. She had flown from New York during the early hours of the morning as soon as she'd heard the news about John. Frank introduced himself, gave his condolences and they then proceeded into the crowded living room.

There must have been twenty people, some sitting, many standing, an assortment of family, friends and colleagues. Beth took Frank over to Mary, who stood talking to a man, who Frank recognised as the Chief of Police.

'Frank,' she said, throwing her arms around him, 'thank you for coming.' Her eyes were bloodshot from the tears she must have cried, her complexion pale as chalk.

'How could I not?' said Frank, 'I'm so very sorry, Mary.' He hugged her tenderly for a moment.

'I'm sorry, have you met police Chief Sanders, Frank?'

'No, I haven't, how do you do – Frank Doyle.'

'Pleased to meet you Mr Doyle. I only wish it were under happier circumstances. How did you know John?'

'We were good friends and we worked in New York homicide together for some years.'

'So, you were a badge? Retired now though I guess?'

'Not quite, I'm a private investigator.' Steve Sanders face expressed disdain.

'Anyway, if you'll excuse me, I'd like a word with Mary, said Frank.' He steered Mary away from Sanders to another part of the room. 'I'm sorry about that, Mary, I didn't come here to talk about me. 'This is a stupid question, but how are you coping, and how are the kids taking it? I said it was a stupid question.'

'I'm numb Frank, I still can't quite believe this is really happening. The kids are upstairs with friends. As you can imagine, they're devastated beyond words.'

'Yes, of course, they will be. Is there someone that's going to stay with you?'

'Beth, my sister, whom you've just met and my parents are coming here from Florida. So you see, I won't be alone. I'll be alright, Frank.'

'Well, just as long as you know, I'm only a telephone call away. If there's anything you need, anything at all, just pick up the phone.'

'Thanks Frank. You must be feeling it as well.'

'Well, yes, yes I am.'

'You were good friends for a very long time, and I know you were always there for him when you worked together.'

The words hit Frank hard. If only he'd been there for him this time, he thought.

'Mary, has John's lieutenant been to see you yet?'

'Sam Rodriguez? He's here now, Frank. That's him stood over there,' she said, pointing the man out. 'Why do you ask?'

'Oh, no reason. Just curious. Anyway, I'd better be going, Mary.'

'Okay, Frank, thank you for coming. I'll be sure to let you know about the funeral,' said Mary, her eyes welling up at the thought.

'Thanks Mary. I'll just say Hi to Lieutenant Rodriguez before I leave if that's okay?'

'Of course, goodbye, Frank.'

'Take care of yourself, Mary,' said Frank.

Rodriguez was in conversation with a couple of uniformed cops when Frank interrupted them.

'Excuse me gentlemen,' said Frank, 'Lieutenant Rodriguez?'

'Yes, that's right. And you are…?'

'Frank Doyle, I'm a friend, was, a friend of John's.'

'Oh, well what can I do for you, Mr Doyle?'

'I was wondering if I could have a word in private?'

'I suppose so. What about exactly?'

'Shall we go outside?'

'If you wish,' he shrugged.

Frank led Rodriguez out to the front garden.

'Now, perhaps you could tell me what this is all about?'

'I'll come straight to the point,' said Frank Brusquely, 'John confided in me the day before he was killed, he was scared. Said he'd had threats. Told to lay off a certain case. Veiled threats they may have been, but threats nevertheless. Know anything about it?'

'I have no idea what you're talking about. What threats? What case?'

'Does the David Ryan case mean anything to you?'

'Uh, yes, a straightforward murder case. Nothing mysterious about it that I remember, just a robbery that went wrong, that's all. What has any of this to do with you anyway?'

Frank didn't answer the question. 'What about the name, Martinez, Hugo Martinez. Does that name mean anything?'

'Look, I don't know who you are, or what your game is, but I advise you to walk away now, Mr Doyle.'

'Is that also a threat?'

'Take it whatever way you want. Just go now, Mr Doyle, before I lose my temper and place you under arrest,' said Rodriguez, his face reddening.

147

'Don't worry, I'm going, but you haven't heard the last of me. You can be sure of that!'

Frank returned to his car, his heart pounding with rage. Yet he felt a certain satisfaction. He had clearly got the man worried and now he was not going to let him off the hook. He seemed as guilty as hell. Frank could almost smell the fear in him.

Chapter Twenty-Three

Frank was aware that he had now placed himself in mortal danger. It seemed to him that John had known the same thing. If Rodriguez was crooked, and it certainly appeared that way, then he would stop at nothing to protect his own interests, even if it meant murdering one of his own men. If he was capable of that, then all things being equal, he wouldn't hesitate to see that Frank also met with the same fate.

He considered the possibility of other cops being on the take from Martinez, the Chief himself, perhaps. Frank had only met him briefly at Mary's home, but he had taken an instant dislike to the man, or was he simply becoming distrustful of everyone? Was the grief he felt for his friend clouding his judgement? He didn't think so.

On his return to his apartment, he dug out his hand-gun from a bedside drawer. From now on, he would keep it on his person at all times. He suddenly felt vulnerable to attack. Not only from Rodriguez, but from Martinez, who he was sure would be told about Frank's further enquiries. Things would have to come to a head soon. Despite his earlier doubts about continuing with the case, the death of his friend made him more determined to bring those responsible to justice.

Stuffing his gun into his jacket pocket, he went downstairs to his office, taking the papers given to him by Alec Mundy, he also inserted the memory stick supplied by Sandra into his computer. He studied the correlation of David Ryan's shift changes with the dates that large sums of cash were deposited into Martinez's bank account, and wondered when his yacht would finally appear back in the port. Without David to safely see it back in, it would be more difficult, Frank thought.

He puffed on his cigar, his thoughts wandering back to John and his bereaved family, when his cell phone rang. It was Sandra Gray.

'Hi Sandra.'

'Hello Frank,' she said. she sounded deeply depressed.

'How are you?' asked Frank.

'Not too good I'm afraid. Frank, I was wondering if we could meet for a drink? I'm going mad stuck in this apartment.'

'Sure, of course we can. I was going to call you anyway. Where would you like to meet?'

'I was thinking O'Malley's, in say, an hour's time.'

'I'll be there,' said Frank.

'Okay, see you soon.'

Frank bundled the papers up from his desk and placed them back in a folder along with the memory stick. He put them back in his filing cabinet and checked his wristwatch. He would be meeting Sandra at 2pm.

On his arrival at O'Malley's, he found Sandra was already there and seated at the bar. She was talking to Danny. Frank approached the bar; he and Sandra exchanged a peck on the cheek and he took the barstool next to her.

'Hi Frank, a beer?' said Danny.

'Yeah, and whatever Sandra's drinking. Oh, and have one yourself, Danny.'

'Thanks, Frank, I'll have a soda.'

'You sounded, unsurprisingly, very down over the phone, Sandra, are you okay?' asked Frank.

'I just needed to get out of the apartment, that's all. I'm okay, really I am.'

'You don't fool me, Sandra. I can't imagine what you're going through. Any luck on the job scene?'

'I've got a couple that I may apply for, but I don't give much for my chances. How about you, Frank, are you okay?'

'Well, no, not great at the moment. I've just lost a very good friend.'

'What, you mean…?'

'Yes, he died in the early hours of this morning. You may have even seen it on T.V. he was a cop; he was shot dead.'

'Oh Frank, I'm so sorry. Yes, I did see it.'

Danny put their drinks down on the bar. Sandra was drinking white wine.

'Do you mind if we grab a table, Sandra?' said Frank.

'No, of course not,' she said, stepping off the barstool.

'I'm afraid there's more to my friend's death than meets the eye,' said Frank, as they walked over to a quiet table.

'What do you mean?' asked Sandra, as they sat down.

'He came to me the day before he died. By all accounts, he'd been asking questions about David's death. It didn't go down well with his boss, who threatened him to keep his nose out of it, or else. A few hours later, he was dead. I think when he and his lieutenant responded to the incident last night, his fate was sealed.'

'Are you saying that your friend's boss is somehow involved with Martinez?'

'That's exactly what I'm saying.'

'It's incredible!'

'Maybe, but I believe it's the truth, and I intend to find out more and nail them.' Frank laughed bitterly. 'I'm not sure how yet, I've still got next to no proof.'

'Just be careful, Frank.'

'Don't worry about me. It's you I'm worried about. Have you had any luck in finding a flatmate yet?'

'Not yet, but I've got someone coming to see me tonight, so…'

'Well, good luck, I hope it works out.'

'Uh, Frank, you mentioned over the phone that you may have something job-wise, that may interest me. What was it exactly?'

'Yeah, well, it was just a thought, but frankly, I don't think you'd be interested. It certainly wouldn't pay well enough, that's for sure, not compared to what you've been used to.'

'I'm pretty desperate, Frank. I'd be interested to know what the job is.'

'Well, it just crossed my mind, that I need an assistant to take care of the office. And well, I thought of you.'

'Really? That would be great, Frank. Thank you. When could I start?' she asked, her mood lifting considerably.

'Whoa, don't let's get ahead of ourselves here. That's the snag, it'd be far too dangerous for you to start until this mess is cleared up. When that happens, I'd be only too glad to have you on-board, even if it were only on a temporary basis. I'm certain something better will come along eventually.'

'Frank, I could kiss you.'

'It's the least I can do.'

I'd like to start as soon as possible, really, I'm a big girl now, I can look after myself. Please Frank, let me start working for you now.'

'Out of the question, Sandra. It's too dangerous. Just wait a little longer, that's all I ask.'

'I can see I'm not going to convince you that I'd be okay, am I?'

'It won't be too long now. Not long at all,' said Frank.

Chapter Twenty-Four

The day after Frank had met up with Sandra, he was meeting a new client whom he had promised to see that day. It was another straightforward matrimonial case. The woman in her forties, believed her husband was having an affair, and after thirty minutes, decided that Frank was the right person to conduct the case for her. She paid him his retainer by writing out a check and left. Frank told her he would begin working on the case as soon as possible.

He was making himself some coffee when he heard someone entering the lobby. He wasn't expecting anyone else. Then came a knock on his office door. He checked his gun that now laid in his desk drawer. He slowly opened the door, to his surprise and somewhat dismay, saw Sandra standing there.

'Sandra, what are you doing here? I thought I told you…'

'Well,' she said confidently, 'aren't you going to ask me in?'

Frank opened the door fully and she stepped inside. She was smartly dressed in a business suit, a smart black jacket with matching trousers.

'It's not that I'm not pleased to see you, Sandra, but what *are* you doing here?'

'Oh, I know you said I couldn't start work straight away, but I thought maybe you could show me what I'd be expected to do once I do start. Please, Frank, I just can't hang around my apartment all day long, it's driving me crazy.'

'I know, but it could be dangerous. I couldn't bear it if something happened, I've caused you enough trouble already.'

'Don't let's go over that again, Frank. None of this is your fault. Now, are you going to let me stay?'

Frank rubbed his chin thoughtfully. 'Well, seeing as you're here – but just for a short while, I'll tell you what the job would entail, then I want you to go home – understood?'

'Okay, whatever you say. Thank you, Frank, it means a lot.'

'Okay then. I've just made some coffee; would you like some?'

'I'll get it, better start off as I mean to go on.' She moved over to where sat a kettle and a couple of mugs. 'Instant coffee?' she said.

'I like it,' said Frank.

'Hmm, better get a coffee maker, you can't offer clients instant.' She perused the office as Frank looked on. 'Not bad,' she said, 'but it could use a feminine touch.'

'Really?' he said, rhetorically.

'First impressions count, Frank.'

'Whatever you say, Sandra – once you start work.'

'Yes, of course.'

Just then the phone rang. Frank let it ring until the answering machine cut in.

'Mr Doyle, this is Sam Rodriguez, we met yesterday. I wonder if we could meet today at around 4pm, let's say at World End, I'm sure you will know it. I'll see you there, Mr Doyle.'

'Was that…?'

'Yes,' said Frank, 'I knew I'd got him worried.'

'Well, surely you're not going? It's a very isolated spot.'

'I'm not about to give up now – yes, I'm going.'

'I'll come with you. I could stay out of sight.'

'The hell you will!'

'But…'

'No buts, Sandra. I'm going alone, that is, except for this,' he said, taking his gun from the desk drawer.

'I don't like it,' said Sandra.

'It'll be fine, don't worry. I'm getting close, Sandra, I can feel it.'

'Yes, maybe you are, but that's no good if you end up like David and your friend.'

The time came for Frank to leave. It was 3pm. Before doing so, he took a small recording device from his desk and placed it in the top pocket of his jacket and of course checked his gun, for now, clicking the safety on.

'Here's a spare pair of office keys,' he said to Sandra, 'lock-up and go home as soon as I've left, okay?'

'Okay,' agreed Sandra.

'Right, I'm ready. I'll speak to you later okay. And don't forget – go home!' said Frank, commandingly.

'I will, I promise,' said Sandra. 'You just take care, that's all.'

'I always do.'

Frank left Sandra in the office as he went to his car parked immediately outside. Sandra's car was a short walk down the street.

Sandra waited a few moments until she saw Frank drive off, switched off the lights and locked the office. She then went to her car as the sky began to darken, it looked as if it was going to rain. She got in and drove away at speed.

By a quarter after three, Frank arrived at the lonely spot with views of Boston and Hingham Harbour. He decided to sit in his car for a while, the sky looked threatening and he could hear the distant rumbling of thunder in the distance. He checked his gun once again and took the safety off. The recording device was ready also. This was the opportunity he'd been waiting for, the chance to get some hard evidence.

Frank was well aware that this may well be a trap of some kind. The location was ideal for a murder, why else would Rodriguez have chosen it? He would have to be truly on his guard at all times, he thought.

It was exactly 4pm when another vehicle pulled up alongside his. He saw Rodriguez get out of his car, Frank did the same, he had already switched on the recorder, he didn't want to miss a thing.

'Shall we walk, Mr Doyle?'

'Okay,' said Frank, subtly scanning the surrounding area.

'Well, Mr Doyle, I didn't think it was the time or place for our little chat yesterday, so excuse me if I seemed rude. I felt it would be much better to continue in private. Don't you agree?'

'If that's what you want. Not quite sure why you chose this place though.'

The thunder was getting closer as they spoke. The sea becoming rougher. Behind them was a wooded area, which Frank kept an eye on at all times.

'Oh, I often come here for some peace and quiet, Mr Doyle.'

'Hmm,' grunted Frank. 'So, what did you want to talk about, lieutenant?'

'What do *you* think I want to talk about?'

'John's murder?'

'Not murder, Mr Doyle. It was a tragic accident, caught in crossfire, plain and simple. As an ex-cop, you should know that these things happen. Yes, I've looked into your background and I also learned that you're now a private investigator. So why don't you stick to unfaithful husbands? – it'd be far healthier for you than poking around in affairs that don't concern you.'

'Sounds like a threat again to me – you were threatening me, weren't you Lieutenant?'

Rodriguez laughed. 'I'm simply telling you to stay out of police business, that's all.'

'You could have done that at the police precinct – why here, if you've nothing to hide? What's your involvement with Hugo Martinez? You are on his payroll, aren't you?'

'Never heard of him.'

'Oh, I think you have,' said Frank.

'You're beginning to irritate me again, I can see I'm not going to convince you, am I, Mr Doyle,' said Rodriguez, looking towards the tree line. Frank noticed his head nod slightly.

At that moment, a car pulled up next to Frank's, now some distance behind them. It was Sandra. 'Frank, watch out! The trees!' she shouted, jumping out of her car.

Chapter Twenty-Five

It all happened in a split-second. Frank dropped to the ground as the bullet from a high-powered rifle sped past overhead. He took his gun from his pocket and looked towards the trees, catching only a glimpse of the gunman fleeing the scene. Frank stood up and turned his gun on Rodriguez who was clutching his left arm. In the confusion, the bullet had found him instead, he was nursing a flesh wound. Rodriguez pulled his own gun from his shoulder holster and pointed it at Frank and backed off, slowly heading back to his vehicle.

'You're not going to shoot, Mr Doyle. You don't have what it takes,' said Rodriguez. 'And you still have no proof of anything.'

'Are you prepared to take that risk?' said Frank.

The stand-off ended as they reached their respective vehicles. Rodriguez opened the door of his car, his gun still trained on Frank.

'I'm going to drive away now, and you're not going to try to stop me. Make no mistake, if you do try – I'll kill you. We're very different people, you and I, Mr Doyle. I won't hesitate to pull this trigger. But I somehow think you would.'

Frank knew the man was right, he watched as Rodriguez got into his car and drove off. He turned to Sandra, standing by her own car, now drenched by the heavy rain.

'Are you okay?' he asked.

'I'm fine, how about you?'

'Well, thanks to you, I'm okay too. I owe you my life, thank you.'

'It was nothing.'

'You took a big risk following me.'

'I just figured you may need some help.'

'And you were right. I did tell you to go home though. It was a foolish thing you did; I can see I'm going to have trouble with you. That said, I'm very very grateful.'

'But what now, Frank? And who do you think was shooting at you?'

'I don't know, but I'm guessing it was one of Rodriguez's men who's also in on the action with Martinez. As to where we go from here, I do have this, at least,' he said, pulling out his recording machine. 'Hopefully, I got everything that was said on here. Come on, let's get out of here.'

'Good idea,' said Sandra, shivering.

The next day, Sandra turned up at Frank's office again, despite being asked to stay away until the case had been brought to a successful conclusion, and until she was no longer at risk.

'Morning Frank,' she said, warily.

'Good morning, Sandra,' Frank said from his desk, 'I thought I told you…'

'Oh, come on, Frank, admit it, you need me. Besides, you can't keep a good woman down.'

Frank shook his head in dismay. 'You're one stubborn woman, Sandra.'

'That's no bad thing, wouldn't you say?'

Frank smiled.

'You know, this is quite a large room. Just an idea, but to look truly professional, we could have a partition wall built so that I could have a desk at the front entrance, rather than clients walking off the street and straight into your office – what do you think?'

'Hmm, yeah, maybe. Anyway, I've got to go out. You mind the store and be careful, okay?'

'Sure. Where are you going?'

'Uh uh, that's on a strictly need to know basis this time.'

'But I do need to know. If I'm going to be your assistant, I need to know these things.'

Frank sighed. 'Okay, if you must know, I'm going to the police headquarters.'

'To see Rodriguez?'

'Not this time, I'm hoping to see the Chief – if he'll see me. I don't think he cares for private investigators very much.'

'Okay, well at least you should be safe there. Keep in touch, Frank.'

'Yes, ma'am,' he said, sardonically, going out of the door.

'I'd like' if possible, to see, Police Chief Sanders,' Frank said to the desk clerk from behind her bullet-proof glass.

'Do you have an appointment?'

'No, I don't,' said Frank.

'Then I'm afraid it won't be possible. If you'd like to make an appointment…'

'Could you just get a message to him that it's about the David Ryan case. I'll wait.'

'What name should I give?'

'Doyle, Frank Doyle.'

'Very well, take a seat.'

Frank took a seat in the marble-floored atrium.

After a thirty-minute wait, the clerk beckoned to him. 'He'll see you now. Wait here and his secretary will be down in a moment to take you up.'

'Thank you.'

As promised, the secretary duly arrived and they took the escalator to the top floor. The secretary knocked on the Chief's door.

'Come in,' he shouted.

'Mr Doyle to see you, sir,' said the secretary.

'I recognize you. You're the private investigator friend of Mary McKay's. I knew the name meant something to me. You'd better come in and take a seat.'

'Thank you, sir. I appreciate you taking the time to see me.'

'Well, what can I do for you? I'm told it has something to do with the Ryan murder. Is that correct?'

'That's quite correct,' said Frank.

'Well, what is it, man?'

'It's a delicate matter, but not to put too fine a point on it, I have reason to believe that at least one of your men was involved in the murder. I also believe the same about John McKay's death, I don't think it was an accident.'

'What! I've never heard such complete nonsense. What the hell gives you the right to come here and accuse my officers of murder, particularly one of their own. I think you'd better leave, Mr Doyle.'

'Hear me out. That's not all. Your Lieutenant Rodriguez asked to meet me yesterday in a very quiet location, it turned out to be an ambush. I was shot at.'

'Mr Doyle, you're trying my patience.'

'Why not get Rodriguez in here. He took a flesh wound by mistake.'

Chief Sanders calmed down a little. 'Very well, if it puts an end to this ridiculous line of questioning.' He called his secretary on the intercom. 'Get Lieutenant Sam Rodriguez up here straight away, will you?'

A few minutes later, Rodriguez arrived in the office. At first, he was shocked to see Frank sitting there. But then he smirked at Frank. 'What's this all about, sir,' he asked the Chief.

'Ask him to show you his left upper arm,' said Frank.

'Very well, Sam, roll up your sleeve,' said the Chief.

'Sure thing, sir.' Rodriguez did as he was asked to reveal a bandage on his arm. He was still smirking at Frank.

'There, what did I tell you?' said Frank.

'Mr Doyle,' said the Chief, 'I have an incident report showing that Lieutenant Rodriguez received that injury at the shooting the other night. The incident where, sadly, John lost his life.' The chief showed him the report. 'Satisfied now?'

'No, I'm not. I also have this recording of our conversation yesterday.' Frank took out his recording machine and played it in its entirety.

'Is that it? That proves absolutely nothing,' said the Chief, 'and now, I think you really had better leave, Mr Doyle, you've wasted quite enough of my time. The Chief and Rodriguez smiled at one another triumphantly as Frank left the office. No one in their right mind could possibly have mistaken the taped conversation as anything other than threatening. It seemed to Frank, that the corruption went to the very top.

Chapter Twenty-Six

Chief Sanders had lied about the injury to Rodriguez's arm. Frank knew the truth, he had witnessed him receiving the flesh wound himself, the incident report had clearly been altered. It seemed that someone was always one step ahead of him and were leaving nothing to chance.

Martinez was bound to be kept informed of Frank's dogged interference and of course the bungled attempt on taking him out of the picture for good. In fact, Frank was counting on it. He wanted Martinez to come after him and try to finish what Rodriguez and his accomplice had bungled. If he could nail Martinez, he could also bring the corrupt cops to justice.

Yes, it would certainly be very risky, but if it brought the whole sordid business out into the open, Frank wouldn't be complaining. Firstly though, he needed to get Sandra away from the office, at least until the danger had passed.

Frank entered his office to find Sandra sitting at his desk, she was just ending a telephone call. 'Hi. Who was that?' he asked.

'A new client,' she replied enthusiastically, 'I found your diary and made an appointment for you to see the lady tomorrow at 10am. Is that okay?'

'Sure, well done. Anything else happened here?'

'No, I tidied your desk up a little, as you can see. I also found this on your desk,' she said, waving a check at him. It was a check for five-hundred dollars made out to from Hugo Martinez. 'Care to explain?' she said, curiously.

'It's a long story, Sandra, I've no intention of cashing that in by the way,' he said, almost apologetically.

'Come on, Frank, you can tell me.'

'Oh well, he offered me work at the casino. It was just a sweetener to get me off his back. I accepted, hoping to gain some information, but it didn't happen, I left after a few days. And that's all there is to it.'

'There, that wasn't so bad, was it?' said Sandra. 'I was just curious, that's all, Frank. Anyway, how did you get on? Did you get to see the Police Chief?'

'Oh yes, I saw him alright. He's as bent as Rodriguez, I'm afraid. I got nowhere.'

'You're kidding.'

'I wish I was. Look, this is getting far too dangerous for you to be here right now. Martinez is bound to come after me again now. I want you out of here.'

'But we make a good team, Frank.'

'I know – I know, but I really must insist that you go home for the time-being. Things are about to get real around here. I just can't risk it.'

'I get the feeling that whatever I say, you're not going to change your mind, are you?'

'No, I'm not, Sandra.'

'Okay,' she said, reluctantly, 'I'll get my things.'

'Okay, thanks, Sandra. It makes sense, you know that don't you?'

Sandra smiled. 'I guess so.'

'By the way, uh, do you need an advance?'

'I'm not quite penniless yet, Frank. There is some good news though. While you were out, I got a reply to my ad for a flatmate, she's coming round tonight for an interview.'

'Oh, good, I hope she turns out to be suitable,' said Frank.

'Hmm, me too. Well, I guess I'll get out of your way. And Frank…' she said as she left.

'Yeah?'

'Be careful.'

Once Sandra had left, Frank secured the office and went up to his apartment, retrieving his gun again from its usual safe place. He stuffed it into his jacket and went out to his vehicle. Lighting a cigar, he drove off to the waterfront.

When he arrived, he walked to the spot where the Martinez yacht should have been moored, yet there was still no sign of it. He decided to walk the half-mile along the waterfront to O'Malley's bar – he needed a drink, a place other than his office or apartment just to think.

He was still determined to nail Martinez and the corrupt police officers, yet he had to admit that just now, there seemed only a slim chance of that happening.

'I don't know what to do,' he said quietly to himself. He ordered another beer from Danny as he arrived at Frank's corner table.

'You okay, man?' said Danny.

'Yeah, I'm fine, Danny. Just tired.'

'Any progress on the case yet?'

'Not enough, I'm afraid.'

'Maybe it was just a random murder, Frank. Maybe David was just in the wrong place at the wrong time.'

'Yeah, maybe,' said Frank, unconvincingly.

Frank's cell phone rang at that moment. Not a number he recognized. 'Excuse me, Danny, I'd better take this.'

'Sure thing, Frank.'

Frank hesitated momentarily before answering. 'Hello,' he said without introducing himself.

'Hello Frank,' came the unmistakeable voice of Martinez. 'How are you? I hope you're keeping well my friend,' he said, mockingly.

'Never mind that,' said Frank, 'what do you want?'

'I must say, that's not very friendly of you, Frank. I was simply concerned about you. I heard you ran into some trouble yesterday.'

'And how would you know that, I wonder?'

'I know everything that goes on in my town, Frank, you should know that by now.'

'Yeah, I'm beginning to get the picture.'

'The thing is, Frank, I've asked you very nicely to stop asking questions, yet you simply haven't listened. It's quite simple, if you can't promise me here and now that you'll stop, then things may get a little uglier. Now I'm sure you don't want that any more than I do, so, may I have your word. The thing is, I like you, Frank. I'd hate to see anything happen to you.'

'Very touching, but I'm afraid the answer has to be no, to you, and your dirty cop friends.'

'That's a shame – a real shame. So, if that's your decision, I'll see you around, Frank.'

The call was not entirely unexpected, yet the words had been chilling. He felt alone against Martinez and the police. There was no one to turn to for help. If there was to be a show-down, it would just be him standing against them.

Frank stayed at O'Malley's 'till late, making his three beers last the entire evening. He paid the tab and left, walking back to his car at the harbour. He felt uneasy walking along the dimly lit waterfront. He checked his gun and returned it into his pocket. As he finally approached Martinez's yacht mooring, a shadowy figure began to approach him. He put his right hand in his pocket where his gun awaited action.

'Frank! Is that you?' came a familiar voice. The shape came closer.

'Who's that?' said Frank.

'It's me, Alec,' the man said, shining his flashlight into his own face. Frank breathed again.

'Jesus, Alec, am I glad it's you.'

'I was going to call you,' said Alec, 'I don't know if it's anything, but we've observed a yacht anchored a way out from the harbour. It's been there for several hours.'

'Interesting,' said Frank.

'As I said, it may be nothing, but I thought I'd let you know. What are you doing here anyway?'

'I was just picking my car up. I was about to go home.'

'Well, listen, it might well be a long time before that craft moves. I'll give you a call if it does. You can count on it.'

'Thanks Alec, I hope it is his yacht.'

'I hope so too, but don't get your hopes up too much, it's not that unusual for a yacht to drop anchor out at sea you know. It may be nothing.'

Frank lit another cigar and drove home, his window wound down. It was a still, cool evening. He hoped there would not be a welcoming committee waiting for him on his return.

Chapter Twenty-Seven

It was 11pm when Frank arrived home. He was confident that no one but him could enter his apartment without the entry system security code. Tapping the four-digit code into the keypad, he entered and switched on the lights. Frank had no intention of sleeping, he made himself some coffee, switched the radio onto WJMX, smooth jazz, switched off the lights and settled down in an armchair next to a window overlooking the street below.

Earlier that evening, Sandra had greeted a potential flatmate, a single woman of a similar age to herself.

'You must be Rachel,' said Sandra, opening her apartment door.

'Yes, that's right, so you are Sandra. I'm pleased to meet you.'

'Pleased to meet you too, please, come in.'

'Nice apartment,' said Rachel, 'it's very cosy, isn't it?'

'I like it,' said Sandra. 'Take a seat. Would you like a glass of wine? I'm having one.'

'That'd be nice, thank you,' she said, seating herself on a large sofa. Rachel was tall with long, bottle blonde hair, well dressed, although not to Sandra's taste, she seemed pleasant enough.

'So, you said over the phone you're a personal assistant. How long have you been in your job?'

'Almost three years now.'

'Anywhere I would know?' asked Sandra.

'I doubt it. It's a very small company.'

'So why are you leaving your present apartment?'

'Well, it's not in a very nice part of town, and this would be much closer to where I work.'

'I see,' said Sandra.

'I have references of course, though I forgot to bring them with me, I'm afraid.'

'Don't worry about that right now, we can sort that out later.'

'So you like what you've see so far?' asked Sandra.

'Yes, very much, I think I could be very happy here.'

'Good. Well, your part of the rent would be $350 a month, plus a share of general expenses. Do you think you could you manage that okay?'

'Oh yes, that's not a problem.'

'Would you like me to show you the rest of the place?'

'Yes, thanks.' Rachel said, placing her wine glass on the coffee table.

They worked their way through the apartment. Firstly, the well-appointed kitchen, the bathroom, Sandra's bedroom, and finally the room that potentially would be Rachel's.

'What do you think of it so far?' asked Sandra.

'It's very nice,' said Rachel. 'Who was here before me?' she asked.

'My partner – he was killed.'

'Oh, I'm sorry – car accident?'

'No, he was murdered.'

'Oh, I'm so sorry,' said Rachel, 'how awful for you.'

'Yes, it was. Well,' said Sandra, quickly changing the subject, 'what do you think, do you think you could live here?'

'Oh, yes, definitely, and I'm sure we'll get along very well.'

'That's great! When do you think you could move in?'

'As soon as possible,' said Rachel, picking up a framed photograph from a wall unit. 'Is this David?' she asked.

A chill ran up Sandra's spine. 'I don't remember telling you my partners name was David,' she said, 'Who are you?'

Rachel slowly replaced the photograph back on the shelf. She turned to Sandra. 'That was very stupid of me,' she said with a half-smile.

'Who are you and what do you want?' shouted Sandra.

Sandra backed away, as Rachel made her way to the sofa where her purse laid. She picked it up and took out a small hand gun. 'I'm not going to hurt you,' Rachel said, pointing the gun at Sandra, 'but I'm afraid you are going to have to come with me,' she said.

'Like hell,' said Sandra.

'Don't make things difficult Sandra. It's a real shame, in a different life, I'm sure we could have been friends – you seem nice.'

'So, I'm guessing you work for Martinez?'

'Kinda.'

'The man who murdered David.'

'I don't know anything about murder,' protested the woman.

'Well, I can tell you he did murder David. Oh, he may not have actually carried it out himself, he's probably too much of a coward for that, but he would certainly have ordered it.'

'And why would he do that?' said Rachel.

'Because he's a monster. David was going to the police to expose him for what he really is, a crook.'

'My Hugo runs a legitimate business. He wouldn't do anything like that,' said Rachel, defensively.

'You must be very naïve. 'What do you suppose he has planned for me?'

'Just to hold on to you for a while, that's all. Come on, let's go,' she said, shaking her gun at Sandra.

It was around 3am when Frank's cell phone buzzed, he woke with a start. He raised himself up from his slumped position and answered.

'Good morning, Frank. Hope I didn't wake you,' said Martinez.

'What do you want, Martinez?'

'Just to let you know that I have someone here with me, someone I believe is rather dear to you. Would you like to speak to her?'

'Put her on!'

'Frank, it's Sandra, I'm…'

'Sandra?'

'I'm okay, Frank. I'm on…'

At that point, the phone was snatched from her. 'Don't worry, Frank, your friend is fine, and she'll stay that way as long as you promise to stay out of my affairs, do you understand? I have some business to attend to, once that's conclude successfully, without interference from you, I'll release her.'

'If you hurt her, Martinez, I swear to God, I'll kill you myself. I could call the police; they could be at your place in minutes.'

'That wouldn't do you much good, Frank, we're not at the casino. Don't worry, you can have her back in just a few short hours, just don't try anything and everything will be just fine. Goodbye Frank.'

Frank paced the floor. He couldn't think straight. Knowing what Martinez was capable of, he knew Sandra was in danger. Martinez was ruthless, and would stop at nothing to get what he wanted. He glanced out of his window and knew immediately he was being watched. In the street lights, he could see a large man sitting behind the steering wheel of a vehicle parked on the opposite side of the street. He couldn't be sure, but it looked very much like Bobby Downes.

Frank's cell phone rang again.

'What do you want now, Martinez?' shouted Frank, angrily.

'Frank, no, it's Alec. Is something wrong?'

'Yeah, there is. Martinez is up to something tonight, I'm sure of it. He's got Sandra.'

'Oh God! And yes, I think you're right. We've been watching his yacht all night and we think something is going down.'

'What's happening?'

'There have been a couple of small launches going back and forward from the yacht. We think they may be unloading, whatever it may be, in an unpatrolled stretch of coastline.'

'Yeah, that makes sense. Alec, I wouldn't mind betting Sandra's on that yacht. I'm coming down, can you meet me there?'

'Sure thing, Frank.'

'All being well, I'll be there in twenty-minutes.'

Frank discreetly peered out of his apartment window once more. The man still sat patiently in his car, waiting for any movement. Once out on the street, he didn't wait for Downes to approach him, instead, Frank walked at pace over to the vehicle. Downes got out, but Frank took him by surprise and pulled out his gun. Downes didn't have time to react. Frank ordered him to turn around and face his vehicle with his hands behind his head.

'You still don't know who you're dealing with, do you Doyle?' said Bobby.

'I know exactly the kind of men I'm dealing with, believe me,' said Frank.

'You won't get very far, you do know that, don't you?'

'We'll see about that.'

Bobby, knowing that Frank wasn't a natural killer like himself, took a chance and quickly turned on Frank. He knocked the gun from Frank's hand and wrestled him to the ground. Bobby was strong and held Frank in a neck-lock from behind as they rolled around. Frank's breathing became constricted, his face reddening, until he found it in himself to strike a heavy blow to Bobby's stomach using his elbow.

It was enough to cause Bobby to release his grip on Frank's throat, he was temporarily winded. Frank pulled himself away and stood up, gasping for breath. He picked up his gun from the road, just as Bobby got up and ran towards him. Frank didn't hesitate, he gave a powerful blow to Bobby's chin, he wasn't expecting it, and it made him reel for a moment.

Taking advantage of the moment, Frank said, 'Sorry about this fella, time to go to sleep,' as he struck Downes across his head with the gun barrel. He slumped onto the roadside unconscious. Frank dragged him to the sidewalk and left the scene in his own car driving fast. Every second counted if he was to be there in time to rescue Sandra.

Frank arrived at the harbour around twenty minutes later to be met by Alec Mundy.

'My boss decided to alert the police on the strength of your information, Frank,' said Alec. 'They've sent out a police launch to patrol any possible landing areas of coast. If they *are* unloading something, then I'm sure they will be picked up.'

'What about the yacht itself?' asked Frank, 'are the police doing anything about that? Sandra may be on it, in fact, I'm sure she is.'

'I haven't spotted any movement there yet, though I'm sure they will.'

'I've got to get out there,' said Frank.

'You can't do that, Frank, it's too dangerous.'

'Watch me,' said Frank, 'with or without help, I'm going.'

'Okay, Frank, you win. I'll speak to my boss.' Alec spoke to his shift supervisor over his radio.

'Out of the question, came a crackly voice. I can't put a member of my staff at risk, absolutely not. We must let the police handle this.'

Frank grabbed the radio from Alec. 'Listen sir, this is Frank Doyle, if you won't let Alec go out there, will you at least allow me to use your boat to go myself. A woman's life is in imminent danger. I can't wait for the police.' There was a long silence.

'Put Alec back on please, Mr Doyle.'

'Yes sir,' said Alec, taking the radio from Frank.

'Very well, if someone's in danger, tell Mr Doyle he can take our small boat out there at his own risk. You, however, stay put, understood?'

'Yes sir, I understand.'

'I take it you heard all that, Frank. Follow me, I'll take you to the boat.'

Chapter Twenty-Eight

Alec took Frank along the jetty, where a small, two-man motor launch was moored. 'Do you know how to operate these things?' asked Alec.

'I'll manage,' said Frank. Light rain was just beginning to fall.

Frank climbed into the boat and Alec cast off. The time was approaching 4am. 'Good luck, Frank, and be careful,' said Alec.

The engine roared into action as Frank switched on the ignition and sped off. The sea was choppy and the craft bounced unevenly on the waves as he made his way to the yacht. Frank had turned the navigation lights of the boat off so as not to alert the yachts occupants. He looked back to shore where the lights of the city twinkled. The journey took him ten minutes, and as he got closer, he killed the engine and drifted towards the gangway at the aft of the yacht.

He quietly secured his craft to the yacht and climbed the gangway ladder. Frank took out his gun and removed the safety, making his way slowly along a catwalk towards the living quarters. He could faintly hear voices coming from inside. It seemed to him that whatever was being moved from the yacht, it had by now all gone, as there was no longer any action taking place. He leant down and carefully looked through one of the windows into what was a large, luxurious cabin.

Martinez sat, laughing and celebrating their operation being a success with a flute of champagne. There were a several other people, some seated, others standing, some of them his heavies, while others, he assumed, were the yachts crew members. There was also a blonde woman sat in the arms of Martinez, while another woman sat with her back to Frank. Her face was obscured, yet he recognised the hairstyle as being Sandra's. He was vastly outnumbered. Were they all armed? Certainly, some would be, he thought. He straightened himself up, wondering what to do next. He would have the element of surprise in his favour, but would that be enough?

Back at the quayside, a plain police car arrived, screeching to a halt. Two detectives got out and flashed their badges at Alec Mundy. 'Are you in charge around here?' one of them asked. 'Well, no, not exactly in charge. My boss is in the office.'

'But you're aware of the situation, right?'

'Yeah, that's right,' said Alec.

'Then you'll do. Okay, give me an update.'

'I'm glad you're here. A friend of mine is being held against her will on a yacht belonging to Hugo Martinez. Well, at least that's what we believe. Also, another friend, an ex-cop, who has been investigating Martinez, has gone out there, and I'm worried. We also think that Martinez has brought drugs ashore. We're not sure where yet.'

'Okay, I'm with you so far. How long has your detective friend been out there?'

'I'd say around twenty-five minutes.'

'Well, there's not much we can do from here. I'll get on the radio to request another police launch to pick us up.'

In the meantime, Police Chief Sanders was at home being kept informed of the situation as it unfolded.

Frank, once again, leaned down to observe through the cabin's window, wondering what action he could take without endangering Sandra. It was then that he felt the unmistakeable cold-steel of a gun barrel touching his neck.

'Get up real slow,' said the man who had crept up on him. He fleeced Frank, found the gun in his pocket and removed it, all the time, keeping his own gun pressed firmly against Frank's flesh. 'Who are you and what are you doing here?' the man asked.

Frank turned his head slightly; he didn't recognize the man. 'I'm here for the girl,' he said firmly.

The man laughed. 'Come with me. I'm sure Mr Martinez would like to meet you – whoever you are.'

'Oh, I'm sure he would,' said Frank.

As they reached the cabin entrance, Frank was roughly pushed inside, his hands behind his head.

'Frank!' cried Sandra.

'Well well well, isn't this cosy,' said Martinez, 'Have you checked to see if he's carrying?' he asked the man.

'He was carrying this. I don't know if he's a cop or what.'

'Oh, Frank's an old friend. Come and take a seat, Frank, join your friend over there.'

Frank reluctantly sat down opposite Martinez. 'Are you okay?' he asked Sandra.

'I've been better,' she said, her forehead furled with anguish.

'So, Frank, tell me how you managed to get past Bobby?' asked Martinez.

'It wasn't too difficult,' said Frank.

'I see. So, where is he?'

'Outside my place, last time I saw him, I'd imagine he's nursing a headache right now.'

'What am I to do with you both?' said Martinez.

'The same as you did to David I assume,' said Sandra, defiantly.

Martinez said nothing, yet his ominous smile, spoke volumes.

'You do realize, don't you, Martinez, the place will be swarming with cops by now. You're finished!' said Frank.

'Not yet, Frank. Besides, aren't you forgetting something? I own the police, at least those who matter.'

'There are still plenty of good cops around, most of them, in fact. Martinez, I repeat – you're finished!'

'Well, we'll see, won't we?'

'Yes, we will,' said Frank.

'Anyway, what do you think of my little yacht?'

'If you really want to know, I think it stinks of dirty money,' said Frank.

'I got this through hard work, my friend, I can assure you.'

'Huh, I doubt you've done an honest day's work in your life, Martinez.'

Martinez's smile dropped. 'Frank, I really don't think you want to annoy me at this point in the game, do you?'

'I don't much care what you think. You'll soon be serving time for murder, and whatever this operation is you have going. I'm thinking drug smuggling.'

'Very good, Frank. Well done!'

'With someone like you, it wasn't difficult. And I'm assuming you get the money cleaned before depositing it into the bank here in Boston?'

'Your talent is wasted on what you do, Frank, it really is. There's absolutely no harm in you knowing now though. Yes, you're correct about the whole shebang, my friend.'

'And Sandra's boss? I wouldn't mind betting she knew what was going on as well. How much were you paying her, I wonder. The same as you were paying Rodriguez and Sanders?'

'You're really very good, Frank. What a waste,' said Martinez, sipping his champagne. 'Tell me, both of you, are you good swimmers?'

Sandra and Frank looked at one another for a moment. They were a long way from the shore. It was then that everyone heard it, the sound of a boat approaching. Frank squeezed Sandra's hand as if to say that it was going to be alright. Martinez and his cronies looked out of the cabin windows, dawn was beginning to break, and through the early sea mist, they could see a police launch nearing the yacht.

For the first time, and much to Frank's delight, Martinez's face started to take on a look of panic. Until then, his demeanour had conveyed an arrogant calmness.

'Looks like the game's up,' said Frank, as the launch settled beside the yacht.

Martinez turned from the window, his face smiling once again. 'Oh, I wouldn't say that,' he said, triumphantly, as two of his men went up to the deck.

Frank was worried, Sandra looked afraid.

A couple of tense minutes passed until Lieutenant Rodriguez and his partner, Jack, also on Martinez's payroll entered the cabin along with the two men that had met them on deck.

'Sam, my old friend, it's good to see you. I knew you'd come,' said Martinez, getting up and shaking his hand.

'Well,' said Rodriguez, 'you have them both, that's good,' he said, looking in Frank and Sandra's direction.

'Frank here, made it all to easy for us,' said Martinez, 'in fact, I was just asking them, how well they could swim,' he said, laughing.

Rodriguez laughed along with Martinez. 'That's too risky, they could get picked up – no loose ends.'

'We could always take them a little further out to sea, just to make sure,' said Martinez.

'Yeah,' said Rodriguez, 'that's not quite what I had in mind.' He and his partner both drew their guns simultaneously. 'Everyone sit – throw your weapons over here, now!'

'What's going on? What do you think you're doing?' said Martinez, jumping to his feet, protesting.

'I said sit.'

Martinez was baffled, yet obeyed. 'I don't understand. What's going on? Do you want more money, is that it?'

'No, no more money. We had a good thing going, but it's over, it's just getting too hot,' said Rodriguez.

'What are you going to do, kill us all?' laughed Martinez, his arrogance displaying again.

'That's the general idea – no loose ends, remember. Sure, we'll have to make it look good, but I'm sure we'll manage.'

'What about us?' asked Frank, 'you'll find it difficult explaining our death's.'

'A tragic accident! You were both caught in the crossfire when we tried to arrest Mr Martinez and his men.'

'Just like John McKay, you mean.'

'Why couldn't you just leave well alone, Mr private investigator? If you had, you wouldn't be in this situation,' said Rodriguez.

'At least let the girl go,' said Frank.

'Well, I'd like to, but no can do, I'm afraid. You see, I get the feeling she might just talk her head off.'

'You can't hope to get away with this,' said Frank.

'Oh, but I will. Now that's enough talking, I need to think,' Rodriguez said, pouring himself and his partner a glass of bourbon from the drink's cabinet.

Chapter Twenty-Nine

Rodriguez and his partner, Jack, took a long slug of bourbon.

'Look, old friend, I'm sure we can work something out,' said Martinez, raising himself to his feet, 'let's talk about this.'

'Sit down!' shouted Rodriguez, the tension beginning to tell.

'How are we going to get out of this one, Frank?' whispered Sandra, leaning into Frank.

'Shut up over there, unless you want to be the first to go,' shouted Rodriguez.

'Lieutenant, I'm not sure I want to part of this anymore,' said Jack, 'I mean, cold-blooded murder, I don't like it. I've got a family.'

'You'll shut up and do as you're told,' said Rodriguez, 'you were quick enough to take the money on offer.'

'That's one thing, but murder…'

'Shut your mouth, Jack.'

'You're right to be worried, Jack,' said Frank, 'There's no hope of walking away from this if you kill us.'

'I'm warning you, Doyle,' said Rodriguez.

Martinez cut in. 'Look, Sam, I'll make you a very rich man if you let me go.'

'Let *you* go! What about *me*?' protested Rachel.

'You really think I give a damn about you? You're nothing.'

'You bastard,' she said, beginning to cry uncontrollably.

'Jesus, can't you tell it's all over. Your operation is finished, Hugo. It's the end of the line,' said Rodriguez.

'It's over for all of you,' said Frank, 'do you remember the recording I played to you and the police chief?'

'What of it?' said Rodriguez.

'I posted it to The District Attorney's office earlier today. It should reach them tomorrow.'

'It proves nothing.'

'Are you willing to take that chance? Especially if you plan to kill us all – it may take some explaining.'

'I've had enough of this,' said Jack.

'Keep your head and we'll be okay,' said Rodriguez.

'No, no more, this is where it ends,' said Jack, kicking one of the guns over to Frank before engaging in a struggle with Rodriguez.

Frank dived onto the floor and grabbed the gun while the two fought. He pointed the gun in the direction of Martinez and his cronies, while picking up another and handing it to Sandra.

'You know how to use one of these, Sandra?'

'Never even held a gun before, Frank,' she said, her spirit lifting.

'Just keep it pointed at them,' said Frank, smiling at her. 'Okay, Rodriguez, drop your gun and sit down over there with the others. Rodriguez and Jack stopped their struggling on hearing Frank's command and did as they were told.

Frank and Sandra moved towards the cabin door. 'We're going to be leaving you now, I got what I came for,' said Frank as they edged out of the door, locking it behind them. They went up to the deck to where the police launch, its motor still running, floated alongside the yacht. Frank was hesitant, was the cop piloting the launch, straight, or was he also on the payroll?

They concealed their guns and hopped on-board.

'Who are you?' asked the uniformed cop.

'My name's Frank Doyle and this is Sandra Gray.'

'Where are the two officers?'

'You know them?' asked Frank.

'Never seen them before in my life, why, what's that got to do with anything?'

'It's a long story buddy. I was a badge myself once. Can you take us back to the harbour and I'll explain on the way? You might also want to call for back-up to pick them all up.'

As they sped off, Frank and Sandra heard the sound of a single gun shot coming from the yacht. Frank and Sandra simply looked at one another without saying a word.

Dawn had broken by the time they reached the harbour. They were greeted by Alec and his boss. The area was now swarming with police vehicles, some of them, black and white's, others, plain cars.

'Thank God you're both okay, said Alec. A sentiment echoed by his boss, who by now had joined him on the waterfront.

'It was touch and go for a while, but, yes, we're fine. Thanks for your help, Alec.'

'What happened out there?' asked Alec.

'I'll explain later, Alec. Right now, I need to speak to the police. Do you know who's in charge?'

'Well, there's a Detective Lieutenant just over there. It looks like he's about to board the police launch that you and Sandra just came back on.'

Frank rushed over to the detective, just catching him before boarding the launch with two other armed officers. 'Lieutenant!' Frank shouted.

'Are you Mr Doyle, the private investigator?' asked Lieutenant Robbins.

'Yes, that's right.'

'Glad you and your friend are okay. What's the situation?'

'Well, as you probably know, they kidnapped my friend, Sandra Gray. Martinez, along with your colleague, Lieutenant Rodriguez who is also on the yacht are responsible for the murder of Sandra's partner and another friend of mine, Detective John McKay. Martinez has a drug smuggling and money laundering operation going – that's why they both had to die, they knew too much.'

'Rodriguez – dirty? He's got twenty years as being a cop, I'm sorry, I can't buy that.'

'If you can't buy that, then you sure as hell won't believe me when I tell you that your Chief Sanders has also been on the take from Martinez.'

'You're right, Mr Doyle, I don't. I'd be very careful about accusations like that if I were you. In any case, the chief is right here overseeing the operation. I don't think he'd do that if he was in any way implicated, do you? Now, if you don't mind, I've got to get out there to see what's going on with my own eyes.'

'Just one other thing. We heard a gun shot as we were making our escape. Be careful.'

'Thanks for the advice,' said the Lieutenant, sarcastically as he and his officers boarded the launch. 'By the way,' he shouted, 'you and your friend will need to come down to the precinct tomorrow to give your statements – just stick to the facts if I were you.'

Frank scoured the various police vehicles and eventually spotted a shadowy uniformed figure sitting in the back of one of them with his driver at the front. He was fairly certain it was the Chief. For a moment, he considered approaching him, but held back the temptation. Instead, he returned to Sandra.

'How are you feeling?' asked Frank.

'I feel good, Frank, glad to be alive. How about you?'

'The same, glad to still be here. You did well out there, Sandra.'

'Teamwork, that's what it was. Say, Frank, what you said about my ex-boss, do you really believe she's involved in this somehow?'

'I can't be certain, but for the large amounts of money passing through his account, it's hard to believe she didn't have some kind of complicity. And if that could be proven, there's a chance you could get your old job back, I guess,' said Frank.

'Hmm.'

'What does, hmm, mean?'

'Oh, nothing,' said Sandra.

'Anyway, all we can do now, is wait for them to return. That is unless you want to go home, I wouldn't blame you after the night you've had,' said Frank.

'You must be kidding. I want to see Martinez brought in.'

Frank chuckled. 'I'll say this for you. You have spirit.'

'Would you both like some coffee?' asked Alec.

'That'd be most welcome,' said Frank.

'I'll go get some from the office,' replied Alec.

Almost an hour passed before the police launch returned. It was tied up, and eventually the figure of Martinez was seen coming down the gangplank and onto dry land. His hands were cuffed as he was escorted from the launch by uniformed cops, he looked an entirely different man to the one Frank had come to know. He took on the appearance of a wholly defeated man.

In quick succession, the other members of his organisation followed suit. Then came Rodriguez's partner, also cuffed. The one person missing, was Rodriguez himself, Frank observed. Frank wondered if the reason for this was the gunshot he and Sandra had heard earlier.

Frank intercepted the Lieutenant as he disembarked. 'Hey, Lieutenant.'

'Doyle, what can I do for you now? thought you would have gone home long ago.'

'You must be joking. I wanted to see Martinez under arrest first. What are the charges?'

'Not that it has anything to do with you, but…'

'Hey,' interrupted Sandra, 'if it wasn't for Frank, you wouldn't have been making any arrests.'

The lieutenant ignored Sandra's remark and continued to talk to Frank. 'As I was saying, we've located the drugs they brought ashore a little way down the coast, so at the moment he's been arrested for illegal importation of cocaine. Does that answer your question?'

'Partly,' said Frank, 'what about Rodriguez?'

'Okay, it does look like you were correct about him. According to his partner, who, by the way, has already admitted to them being on Martinez's payroll, Rodriguez shot himself in the temple at close range. Now if you'll excuse me, I've got to arrange for forensics to get out to the yacht, and the Chief is coming over, I have to report to him.'

'As I said, he's involved too. But don't take my word for it, examine his bank account,' said Frank.

The Lieutenant appeared to ignore his advice and liaised with the Chief. The Chief had a worried expression and gave a passing glance of distain in Frank's direction.

'If looks could kill,' Frank thought aloud.

Chapter Thirty

'I'll take you with me! I swear to God,' came a shout form Martinez as he was being bundled into one of the police vehicles.

'Martinez seemed to be talking to you, Chief,' said the perplexed Lieutenant, 'Was he talking to you?'

Frank, who had heard the accusing cry from Martinez, cut in. 'Oh yes, he was talking to him alright, isn't that right, Chief Sanders?'

'Don't listen to him, Lieutenant, he's talking nonsense. I don't even know this man.'

'Well, seeing as how I was in your office just the other day, I'm sure your secretary would be glad to verify that we did in fact meet,' said Frank.

'Is that right, Chief?' asked Lieutenant Robbins.

'Are you questioning my honesty Lieutenant?' said the Chief.

'To be honest sir, I'm not sure of anything at the moment. But we already have a cop under arrest, plus Rodriguez, who it seems took his own life rather than face the shame. All I can say is, this man has been right about everything so far, so...'

'You can't take Doyle seriously, he's nothing but a small-time…'

There was a moment's silence between the men. 'So, you do know him then?'

'I – I.'

'I'm sorry Chief, I'm going to have to take you in,' said the Lieutenant.

'You're not taking me anywhere,' said the Chief, drawing his gun.

'Don't be a fool, sir.'

'I can't go to prison, understand.'

'Let's just talk it over, okay?'

'No! I'm leaving now and don't try to stop me. As for you,' he said, turning his attention to Frank, I've half a mind to kill you where you stand, you meddling bastard. Who's going to miss a two-bit private detective.'

'Where's that going to get you?' said Frank, 'just like Martinez – you're finished, Sanders.'

The Chief began to back off and make his way to his car. He pointed the gun at his driver and told him to get out of the vehicle. Then, taking his place at the wheel, sped off.

Lieutenant Robbins, calmly ordered a black and white to pursue, knowing the Chief would not get far. He followed in his own vehicle.

Frank and Sandra approached the car that Martinez sat forlornly in the back of with a uniformed cop by his side, guarding him. He gestured to the cop to open the window.

'Looks as if you won this time Frank,' Martinez said, regaining some of his arrogance, 'however, I'll be out in a year or two, and I want you to know, I have a very long memory.'

'You'll need a long memory once they've proved that you orchestrated the murder of David Ryan, and most likely my friend, John McKay. You're going away for a very long time Martinez,' said Frank. 'Oh, and let's not forget the kidnap of my associate.'

Martinez simply laughed as Sandra moved closer. She slapped his face hard, his expression returning to one of defeat.

'That felt so good, Frank,' she said, triumphantly.

'I bet it did,' said Frank, chuckling, 'Come on, let's get out of here. I'll buy you breakfast.'

Lieutenant Robbins and his uniformed colleagues finally caught up with Chief Sanders at Police Headquarters. He rushed inside the building, making his way to the elevator. The Lieutenant and his men followed, but the Chief had already began ascending to the top floor. All they could do was wait to recall the elevator. It seemed to take forever.

'To hell with this,' said Robbins, 'let's take the stairs.'

They reached the fourth floor, breathless. Catching their breath, they all drew their guns before cautiously entering Chief Sanders substantial office. They found him sitting behind his desk, gun in hand. He didn't, as expected, wave his gun at them, but instead, sat upright in his office chair in what could only be described as a dignified position.

'It's over, sir,' said Robbins, 'I'm going to have to ask you to come with us. You're under arrest,' he said, sombrely.

'Can I ask what the charges are?'

'Accessory to the murder of John McKay.'

'I see,' said Sanders, straightening his tie, 'It would seem I have no more cards to play.'

'That's right, sir, you don't.'

'Can I at least have a couple of moments to call my wife?' asked Sanders.

'That'd be most irregular – I'll give you three minutes, okay. We'll be right outside the door. Oh, and I'll take that,' said Robbins, gesturing to Sander's gun.

'Of course,' said Sanders, with a weak smile.

Robbins took the gun. 'Three minutes!'

The group left the office and stood, listening at the door.

The Chief straightened his uniform jacket and his tie once again, opened his desk drawer and took out his personal gun. He didn't hesitate, he thrust it in his mouth and pulled the trigger.

Robbins and his men rushed in. 'Ah, Jesus,' he said, turning his head away momentarily. Blood and brain tissue dripped from the wall behind the Chief's desk. He lay slumped in his chair.

'Goddammit! Two cops commit suicide in one day. What a day! I'm gonna be up to my neck in paperwork for a month. Get a forensics team up here now, will you?' he said, turning to one of the uniformed officers.

'Will do, Lieutenant. Don't blame yourself, sir, you were just trying to do the decent thing.'

'I should have known better. But thanks anyway.'

After many hours of questions and giving their written statements, Frank and Sandra left the police precinct. They had also been given the news about the Police Chief.

'I'll say this, Frank, there's never a dull moment with you around. The past 24 hours has been quite something. I'll never forget it, that's for sure,' said Sandra.

'Me neither, Sandra. I'll drive you home, it's been a long day,' said Frank.

'Actually, Frank, would you mind if I slept on your sofa? It just feels a little weird going back to my apartment tonight. Just for one night! I'm sure I'll be okay after that.'

'I'll do better than that, I'll make up my bed for you and I'll take the sofa.'

'I can't ask you to do that, you must be exhausted.'

'I insist,' said Frank.

'Thanks Frank, thanks for everything. Martinez would still be free if it wasn't for you.'

'Well, we won't be seeing him again, except perhaps in court. 'Let's head back to my place then and grab something to eat before having a well-earned rest.'

'Good idea. How long do you think he'll get, Frank?'

'Martinez? Long enough so that you'll never to have to worry about him ever again,' said Frank.

'I hope you're right.'

'Trust me, he's not going to walk away from this one.'

It was around 9.30pm when Frank's doorbell rang. Sandra was taking a shower before they sat down to eat the takeout pizza that Frank had ordered twenty-five minutes earlier.

'Looks like our pizza has arrived, Sandra,' shouted Frank.

'Okay, I'll be right there,' she shouted back.

Frank approached the door. 'Who is it?'

'Pizza delivery,' came the voice of a young man.

Frank opened the door to briefly glimpse the terrified delivery boy before he was shoved through the doorway and into the apartment. It happened in seconds. The next thing Frank knew was the giant shape of Bobby Downes following immediately after, he was carrying a switchblade.

'Stand over there out of the way, son,' said Frank to the delivery boy. I have to admit, I'd forgotten about you, Downes,' he said, backing away. This won't do you any good, your boss and the rest of the gang have all been arrested.'

'I know,' came the low, gruff voice of Bobby Downes.

'So what do you want? It's all over.'

'You've taken away my livelihood. What do I want? I want your heart on a plate.'

Downes moved menacingly closer, the blade pointing at Frank.

'Hey, what's all the commotion?' shouted Sandra, making her way from the bathroom.

Downes was momentarily distracted. Frank lunged at him, grabbing the hand that held the blade. They struggled and both tumbled onto the floor. Downes found himself on top of Frank, pinning him to the floor while he tried to force the blade downwards. It took all of Frank's strength to keep it from plunging into his chest. Sandra grabbed an ornament, and approaching from behind Downes, smashed it over his head. It dazed him for a moment, but didn't stop him.

The pizza boy made his escape and ran out of the apartment. Sandra picked up another, heavier ornament and once again, found her target on Downes's head, it smashed into several pieces on his hard skull. He simply shook his head and carried on, the switchblade getting closer and closer to Frank's body.

'Frank, where's your gun?' screamed Sandra.

Frank found it difficult to answer during the struggle, yet he just managed to say, 'the bedside cabinet. Hurry!'

Frank managed to roll Downes over onto his back, giving him a momentary advantage. Yet Downes still found the strength to push the knife closer, until it found Frank's arm, piercing through his shirt until blood appeared. Downes grinned with pleasure. Frank let out a gasp of pain and was again rolled onto his back. Downes freed his hand and raised the knife ready to plunge it into Frank's chest.

'Hold it, or I'll shoot, so help me God,' shouted Sandra. Downes was to frenzied to take any notice. He raised the blade higher still and paused as if for effect. 'This is your last chance,' she said, 'I'll shoot.'

Downes glanced at her for a second with an evil grin and began to plunge the knife. Sandra took aim, pulled the trigger and shot him once in the back. The knife fell from his grip and his body fell on top of Frank.

Frank pushed him aside. He was clearly dead.

'Boy am I glad you stayed tonight. You did good,' said Frank.

Chapter Thirty-One

Three Weeks Later.

Things were beginning to look better for Sandra. She had at last found a suitable flatmate, the two had hit it off from the get go and were close in age. They shared many of the same interests and taste in music, they just got on well together.

Sandra had been contacted by the Chief Executive of the bank and offered her old job back, albeit in a slightly less senior position. Her actions had been fully vindicated. Karen, her old boss was suspended and under investigation for complicity. Sandra was told that Karen may even face criminal proceedings. The news made her sad that someone she had known and worked with for so long could be involved with the likes of Martinez – the man ultimately responsible for David's death, simply through greed and the desire for power.

'I'm going to work now Emily, see you this evening,' Sandra called to her new flatmate who was in the bathroom.

'Okay, see you later. Have a good day,' she replied.

It was a big day for Sandra, her first day at a new desk.

Driving to work, she found herself in a reflective mood. She was certainly happier than she had been for a number of weeks, but couldn't help thinking about David, about Martinez and of how Frank had gone to such lengths, and had put his own life in danger several times to solve the case. As she stopped the car, she glanced at the photograph of David that she had blue-tacked to the dashboard and smiled.

She entered the office and sat at her brand-new desk, complete with computer, telephone and a pleasant waiting area, she was eager to start work. Sandra went through a connecting door to where sat her new boss.

'Good morning. Coffee?' she asked, breezily.

'Oh yes please,' said Frank, 'I can't work that new fangled machine you have out there.'

'*You*, don't have to, that's my job now,' said Sandra.

'So, what do you think of your office,' asked Frank.

'It's great, Frank, just how I imagined it.'

'Before you get our coffee, sit down for a moment,' said Frank.

'Okay.'

'Are you a hundred percent sure about this, Sandra? I mean, you're sure this is what you want to do?'

'I'm two-hundred percent sure, Frank. That is on one condition.'

'And what's that?'

'Come on now Frank, you know what I'm talking about,' Sandra said with a smile, 'that I'm not just a secretary, remember?'

'Oh that.'

'Yes, that! I want to be involved in some of the cases you take on – I think I've proved to you I can handle myself.'

'You certainly have, I can't argue with you on that,' said Frank.

'Then do we have an agreement?'

Frank extended his hand across the desk. 'We have an agreement,' he said.

The End.

Printed in Great Britain
by Amazon

78544677R00121